Margaret Tempest.

NEWBY
HALL

This book belongs to

Fiona Campbell

Christmas 1982.

LITTLE GREY RABBIT'S
SECOND STORYBOOK

LITTLE GREY RABBIT'S
SECOND STORYBOOK

by Alison Uttley

PICTURES BY
MARGARET TEMPEST

COLLINS St James's Place, London

William Collins Sons & Co Ltd
London · Glasgow · Sydney · Auckland
Toronto · Johannesburg

Uniform with this volume
LITTLE GREY RABBIT'S STORYBOOK

First published in this edition 1981
Reprinted 1982
© This collection text Alison Uttley Literary Property Trust 1981
© This collection illustrations Margaret Tempest 1981
ISBN 0 00 194163 1
Made and Printed in Hong Kong by
South China Printing Co.

Contents

Squirrel Goes Skating

Everything was frozen. Even the brook which ran past little Grey Rabbit's house on the edge of the wood was thick with ice. Each blade of grass had a white fringe, and the black leafless trees were patterned with shining crystals.

On every window of the house were Jack Frost's pictures, – trees and ferns and flowers in silver. Little Grey Rabbit stood looking at them with delight, wishing they would always be there, in Summer as well as Winter.

"Grey Rabbit! Grey Rabbit!" called Hare as he came downstairs in his brown dressing-gown. "Put some more wood in the fire. It's bitter cold to-day." He shivered as a draught blew under the door and ran round his feet.

Grey Rabbit left the window and put a log on the fire. She pulled the table closer and drew up the chairs.

"I believe I've got a chilblain," said Hare in a complaining voice, as he examined his toes. "Yes, I thought so. It's a big chilblain! What can you do for it, Grey Rabbit?"

The little Rabbit went to the medicine cupboard and looked at the bottles which stood in a row.

There was Primrose Wine for coughs and colds and feast days, and Venom for Dangerous Visitors, and Dandelion for toothache, and Dock leaves for bruises, St. John's Wort for cuts, and nothing for chilblains.

"There isn't anything for chilblains," said Grey Rabbit sadly.

"Ow! Ow!" exclaimed Hare, rubbing his toe. "Do think of something, Grey Rabbit. You don't know how it hurts!"

"Moldy Warp once told me to use snow. I'll get some."

She ran outside and scraped the rime from the grass. Then she rubbed Hare's foot till the chilblain disappeared.

"Grey Rabbit! Grey Rabbit!" called Squirrel, coming downstairs with a shawl over her shoulders. "Pile up the fire and keep out the cold. You've had the door open this frosty morning, and let the North Wind in. Drive it out!"

So Grey Rabbit put another log on the fire, and sent away the little wind which had rushed in when she went out.

"I believe my paw is chapped," said Squirrel, holding

it out for a snow rubbing.

At last they sat down to breakfast, with hot tea and thick buttered toast, and carrot sausages.

"Milk-o," called a voice, and Hedgehog knocked at the door.

"It's fruz to-day," said he, as he turned a solid lump of milk out of his can.

"I went to the cow-house – it's the only really warm place on a day like this – but icicles hung all round my little door, and nearly stabbed me as I went in."

He was indeed a queer sight, with his prickles all frost covered, so that he looked like a spiky snowball.

"Come in, and warm yourself, do, Hedgehog," said Grey Rabbit hospitably.

He stamped his feet at the door, rubbed them on the mat, and tip-toed over to the fire. Squirrel chopped off some of the milk and put it in the tea, and Grey Rabbit gave a cup to the frozen Hedgehog.

As he sipped from his saucer, blowing and puffing at the steam, he talked.

"There's skating over Tom Tiddler's way," said he, "and I've heard tell that every one is going. Moldy Warp was trying on his skates as I came past his back door, and I met a couple of Brown Rabbits with their toboggan."

Hare put down his knife and fork.

"Let's go too," said he. "Hurry up, everybody, and Hurrah for Skating!" He gobbled up his breakfast as fast as he could.

"There's no hurry, Mr. Hare," drawled Hedgehog. "Ice'll wait. There'll be no thaw this side Christmas, I can tell 'ee that from the looks of the moon." And he took another sip of his tea.

"Moldy Warp's gone, Brown Rabbit's gone, and Hare ought to have been the first," mumbled Hare with his mouth full.

"Well, I must be getting on," said Hedgehog, wiping his mouth with his spotted red handkerchief. "Thank ye kindly for the tea." He tiptoed out again, leaving a little stream on the floor.

Grey Rabbit wiped it away, and Hare jumped up from the table. "Have you ever seen me skate?" he asked. "I'm a very good skater. It's in me to skate. I am a born skater, just as I'm a born adventurer."

"And a born boaster," whispered Squirrel to the teapot.

"Did you ever hear how I skated round Lily Pond backwards, and passed all the other skaters forwards? I'll tell you about it."

"Not now," said Grey Rabbit gently. "We must get our skates cleaned, and the house tidied, and make the beds, pack the lunch and lock the door."

"And brush our tails and put on our best clothes," added Squirrel. "All the world will be there."

Hare went out to clean the skates, Squirrel disappeared upstairs, and little Grey Rabbit did everything else as quickly as she could. She washed the dishes, and

swept the floor, she made up the fire, and chopped the sticks for the next day, she dusted the kitchen and made her bed, she cut the sandwiches and packed them in the basket.

She even remembered to put in an extra loaf for any hungry Rooks who might be on the ice.

When she stood ready to go, neat as ever in her grey dress with its clean collar and cuffs, and a little muffler round her neck, she called Hare and Squirrel.

"Hare, are you ready? Hare!"

Hare came running in, with a basket full of icicles. "I've been collecting these, to take for drinks," said he, excitedly. "You just suck one like this" – and he held one in his mouth – "and it makes a nice watery drink."

"That's splendid," said Grey Rabbit, "but I think we ought to take the kettle too, because somebody might like a hot drink."

"And a lemon," added Hare, "for hot lemonade."

"But you haven't changed your dressing-gown! Are you going to skate in it? And where are the skates?"

"Oh, Jemima!" exclaimed Hare. "I forgot the skates and my dressing-gown." And he hurried off to get ready.

"Squirrel! Squirrel! Are you ready? We're going," called Grey Rabbit at the foot of the stairs.

"Coming in a moment," said Squirrel, and Grey Rabbit took a last look round. The table was laid ready for their return, when they would be tired, hungry, and happy. There was a herb pie, an apple tart, some jam puffs, and cob-nut cutlets.

The rabbit smiled the contented smile of the good house-keeper. "I'll put out a bottle of Primrose Wine for the festival," said she, trotting to the larder.

"Can you come here?" called Squirrel in a muffled voice. Grey Rabbit and Hare both hurried to Squirrel's room.

A strange sight met their eyes.

A green dress was jumping round and round the room, with two little paws waving wildly in the air. A green beribboned tail stuck half-out of one of the sleeves, and Squirrel was so hopelessly entangled that her head couldn't find a way out at all.

Hare and Grey Rabbit sank down on the bed helpless with laughter, as Squirrel turned like a spinning top. When at last they straightened her out they found she had decked herself with little green bows on her ear-tufts, and hung a locket round her neck.

"Oh, Squirrel, you cannot go like that!" said Grey Rabbit. "Like a Mummer at a Fair," added Hare rudely. So Squirrel untied her ear ribbons, but she insisted on keeping the ribbon on her tail, and the locket round her neck, and the bows on her dress.

Off they went at last, Grey Rabbit carrying the basket of food, Hare swinging the basket of icicles in one paw and the kettle in the other, and Squirrel following daintily with the skates dangling on her arm.

They locked the door, and put the key on the window-sill. Over it they sprinkled leaves and grass with a few icicles to give a natural touch.

"Nobody would guess that was a key," said Hare, and the others agreed.

The world gleamed like a sparkling diamond, and the air was fresh and sweet as spring water. The three animals ran down the lane and across the fields towards Tom Tiddler's Way.

"No going through the Wood to-day," laughed Hare.

"I wonder how Wise Owl is," said Grey Rabbit.

"I heard him out hunting last night," said Squirrel, "and his voice sounded rather croaky. He said, 'Too-whit, it's cold. Too-whoo, it's freezing.' And I said, 'Try a hot-water bottle, Old Thing.'"

"Oh! Did he hear you?" gasped Grey Rabbit.

"No. I said it under the bedclothes," answered Squirrel, with a chuckle.

Little hurrying footsteps came along a side path, and a party of Brown Rabbits, each with a pair of skates hanging on his back, joined them.

"Fine day, Squirrel! Fine day, Grey Rabbit! Fine day, Hare!" said they. "Going skating?"

"No, we're going flying," snapped Squirrel, who did not want their company.

The Brown Rabbits nudged each other and walked behind.

Hare led the way, past Moldy Warp's house, through the fields where Grey Rabbit had picked primroses for

wine in the Spring, under the leafless hedgerows and the tall bare trees.

"Stop a minute," called a voice as they crossed a frozen stream, and a handsome Water-rat joined them. He wore a brown velvet coat with snow-white frills, which were laundered by the homely Water-hens every day, he was so particular.

"It's not often I get the chance of such fine company," said he, smiling at Squirrel. "Are you going to the Fair, Miss Squirrel?"

"I'm going skating," answered Squirrel, demurely giving her bows a twitch.

"Oh, I beg your pardon, I thought you were going on the round-abouts," said the Water-rat mischievously.

Grey Rabbit was an old friend of his. They had often met when Squirrel was out marketing near the stream.

He showed her where the best water-cress and spring cabbage grew. He was a great talker and a friend to many animals.

"I had such an adventure the other day," he began.

"Adventure," called Hare over his shoulder. "Adventure, did you say? You should hear about my great adventure." But the Water-rat took no notice and went on with his tale.

"I followed the stream for miles and miles just for fun. I thought I would go on till it got to the sea, but when it reached a broad river I felt tired and decided to go back home. I noticed a nice house by the river bank, under the roots of a fine willow tree, with the door on the latch, so I pushed the door open, very quiet-like, you know, for I didn't wish to be taken for a burglar, like those thieving rats. I wanted to see who lived within, and the kind of furniture they had, and how many they were in a family. You understand?"

"Yes, we understand," said the Brown Rabbits, crowding near to him, and Hare and Squirrel also pressed closer.

"I just poked my nose in, and there, sitting on each side of the hearth, sat Mr. and Mrs. Otter, and on the floor was a young Otter, playing with a box of bricks. He saw me and cried out, and I ran, and ran, and ran."

"That was a narrow escape!" exclaimed Hare. "It only shows you shouldn't poke your nose in other people's houses. Now when I was in Fox's house—"

"Oh, we've heard that story," interrupted the rabbits.

"Very well," said Hare, in high dudgeon. "I was only going to say I played noughts and crosses, and if Water-rat learned to play he might get out of the scrapes into which his fine swimming takes him." And Hare cuffed the nearest rabbit on the ears.

By this time they had reached the pond, which lay in the centre of a small field, with slender willows and crooked alders leaning over it, making seats and swings for those who didn't skate.

Already many animals were on the ice, and the air was filled with merry cries, with squeaks, and laughter. The newcomers sat down on the bank and put on their skates. Grey Rabbit placed her basket of food in the care of Mrs. Hedgehog, who sat on a log of wood, watching her son, Fuzzypeg.

Soon they were laughing and shouting with the others as they skimmed over the ice. Squirrel caused some excitement as she went by with her bows and ribbons flying, and some whispering among the girl rabbits.

Hare tried to do the outside edge, and got mixed up with the skates of a White Duck. He fell down with a thump and bruised his forehead.

"Grey Rabbit! Grey Rabbit!" he called. "Grey Rabbit! I've bumped myself." And Grey Rabbit ran up and rubbed him with her paw. She dusted the powdered snow off his blue coat, and helped him to his unsteady feet.

"Kind little Grey Rabbit," murmured Mrs. Hedgehog approvingly, as the rabbit went to some young brown rabbits who were in difficulties. Every time they started off, one of them sat down, and tumbled into the others, so that they were a continual bunch of kicking legs.

Grey Rabbit and Water-rat linked paws with them and steered them across the pond, to their joy and happiness. Away they went, ears back, heads up, fur stiff in the wind, their eyes shining and their breath coming and going in little pants, as their tiny feet glided over the ice.

Moldy Warp was there, skating as well as he did everything else, slow and sure, round and round, picking up the fallen, avoiding Hare's wild dashes, giving a kindly word here and there.

"I'm hungry," called Hare. "Let's have lunch." So they returned to Mrs. Hedgehog, who still sat with her eyes on young Fuzzypeg and on no one else.

Grey Rabbit unpacked the basket, and Squirrel invited Water-rat, Moldy Warp, Mrs. Hedgehog and her son to join them. There was enough for all, and still there was a loaf left for the crowd of hungry black-coated rooks who loitered on the pond's edge, offering to put on anyone's skates for a groat.

Hare's icicles were very thin by now, but he handed round the basket and each sucked the sweet cold ice. The rooks collected sticks for a fire, and soon Grey Rabbit had the kettle boiling and hot drinks of lemonade for all the company.

"Sour! Sour!" grimaced little Fuzzypeg, but his mother nudged him to remember his company manners.

They all returned to the ice and skated until the red sun set behind the far hills, and the air took on a new fresh coldness. The sky was violet, and the dark shadows spread across the fields, as the animals removed their skates and set off home.

"It has been a jolly day," said Grey Rabbit to Water-rat and Moldy Warp. "Good-bye. Perhaps we will come again to-morrow."

"Good-night. Good-night," resounded round the pond. "Good-night," echoed the trees, and soon the little white paths under the black hedges were crowded with small animals hurrying home to field, burrow, cot, and cave.

"Did you see me skate?" asked Hare excitedly. "I did the double-outside-edge backwards and figure seven on one leg."

"I saw all the little rabbits and field mice you knocked down," said Squirrel severely.

Grey Rabbit cried, "Hush! Don't make a noise at night. Wise Owl doesn't like it." So they walked softly along, and the stars came out to keep them company.

The key was on the window-sill, under the pile of grass, but there were footprints in the garden.

"Someone's been here whilst we've been skating," said Squirrel, looking anxiously up and down. "It isn't the milkman or the postman."

They all hurried inside the little house, and stared in dismay at the sight. On the table lay the remains of the feast for three, only bones and crusts and an empty bottle of Primrose wine!

"Oh! Oh!" cried Hare. "I was so hungry, and there isn't enough for a bumble-bee."

"Oh! Oh!" cried Squirrel. "I was so thirsty, and there isn't a drink for a minnow."

"Oh! Oh!" cried Grey Rabbit. "I left such a feast, and now look at the dirty table-cloth and the broken dishes and the spilt wine! It's as bad as the Weasel's house."

"Oh! Who's been here since we've been gone?" they said all together, running to the larder.

Not a scrap of food remained! All the eggs, the nuts, the onions, the tea and the flour had gone, and over the floor were footprints, ugly footprints.

They opened the door at the bottom of the flight of stairs and ran softly up to the bedrooms, each with a little candlestick and a tiny candle.

"There's no one in my attic," whispered Grey Rabbit, as she peered in her room, which was neat and tidy as she had left it.

"And there's no one in my room," said Hare, more boldly, picking up the brown dressing-gown he had flung on the floor when he went out in the morning.

"Oo-Oo-Oo," squeaked the Squirrel. "Somebody's sleeping in my bed! Oo-Oo-Oo." And she nearly dropped her candle in her fright.

They peered through the open door, but all they could see was a long, thin tail hanging down on the floor and long black whiskers sticking out of the sheets.

"Who is it?" whispered Squirrel in a trembling voice. "It's Rat's tail," said Hare. "I remember when I met him under the hedge one night, with his bag on his back, I saw those little rings round it."

"They're Rat's whiskers," said Grey Rabbit, below her breath.

"Then it must be Rat himself," sobbed the poor

Squirrel.

They tiptoed up and looked at the lump under the sheets and listened to the snores which came from the comfortable Rat. Then they tiptoed downstairs, each with a candle dropping tallow on the steps, they were so alarmed.

"What shall we do?" they asked each other, as they stood in the untidy kitchen.

Hare trembled so much that the candle fell out and burnt his paws.

Squirrel forgot to use her handkerchief in her agitation and wiped her streaming eyes on her beribboned tail.

Grey Rabbit shivered as she thought of Rat's sharp teeth.

But no sound came from the bedroom except the long snores, and in a few minutes the little animals were less alarmed.

"I'm very good at catching foxes," said Hare boldly, "but I don't remember how to catch a Rat."

"I once caught a Weasel," said Grey Rabbit shivering, "but I couldn't catch a Rat."

"We don't want to catch him," said Squirrel. "He's caught already. We want him to go out of my bed."

The others looked at her in surprise and admiration. "Let's shoo him out," she continued.

"But he ought to be punished," objected Grey Rabbit. "We ought to make him remember his wickedness."

"When I want to remember anything I tie a knot in my handkerchief," said Hare.

"But I don't think Rat has a handkerchief," said Grey Rabbit.

Then Squirrel spoke these astonishing words, "I can tie knots," said she. "I can tie ribbons and bows. I often tie my knitting to keep the stitches from falling off the needles and getting lost. I will tie a knot in Rat's tail, and it will never, never, never come undone. Then he will never, never, never forget his wickedness."

"Will the ribbon never, never, never, come undone, that you tied on your own tail?" asked Hare innocently. But Grey Rabbit frowned and told him to be quiet.

Squirrel crept upstairs again and Hare and Grey Rabbit followed with a candle to light her in her task.

She picked up the long tail, and tied and twisted it and turned it, and doubled it, and looped it, and twined it till it made one great knot which nobody could ever unfasten, and the Rat never awoke, for he had eaten so much and drunk so much from the little Grey Rabbit's larder.

They shut the door and ran downstairs with beating hearts.

"Now we must frighten him away," said Grey Rabbit, "for we don't want him to stay here always."

Hare took the tongs and poker, Grey Rabbit took two saucepan lids, and Squirrel took the bundle of skates. They hammered and banged against the bedroom door, and made such a clang and clatter, such a rattle and racket, such a jingle and jangle, that the Rat awoke.

He sprang out of bed, bewildered, opened the window, and jumped out on to the flower-bed below.

"Whatever's that a-bumping and a-clumping behind me?" said he to himself, and he turned round to find his tail in a knot.

He ran down the paths with the knot reminding him of his wickedness all the way, and he didn't like it at all. It was most uncomfortable to be reminded continually of his sins.

At last he sat down and tried to undo the knot, but just then Wise Owl came sailing along the sky, over the meadows and woods. He spied Rat down below, twisting and turning, as he tried to unfasten his tail.

"Hello, Rat!" said he, and he flew down to look at the unfortunate animal. "Hello! Been in mischief? There's a proverb in the Book of Owlish Wisdom hanging on my tree. It is: 'Many go out for wool and come home shorn.' Learn it, Rat! Learn it!"

He chuckled in a goblin way, which made Rat shiver, and then soundlessly rose from the bough and flew away.

"Come home shorn," echoed Rat mournfully, as he hobbled along.

In the little house Grey Rabbit put clean sheets on Squirrel's bed, and Squirrel swept the floor, and Hare made a fire in the kitchen to cheer everybody up as there was no food.

Suddenly there came a knock at the door.

Thump! Thump! Thump!

The three animals looked at one another. "Is it Rat come again?" they asked anxiously.

Thump! Thump! Thump! "Grey Rabbit! Open the door," cried a voice.

"That's Mole," said Grey Rabbit happily, and she flung wide the door.

"Moldy Warp, we are so glad to see you," she cried as Mole staggered in with a big hamper, followed by Water-rat with another.

"I thought we could end the skating day with a feast," said Mole, "so I came along with a few provisions."

They both opened the baskets and took out a dozen eggs, some buttered tea-cakes, a Bakewell tart, and a cranberry jelly, some raspberry jam and dandelion sandwiches and a big plum cake with icing on the top.

"Hurrah!" cried Hare. "Hurrah!" said Squirrel. "Talluraley!" sang little Grey Rabbit, dancing round the room.

"Hedgehog is bringing an extra can of milk," said Mole. "I thought you might be short. In fact," he continued, winking, "somebody whispered that you had had a visitor to-day, an unwelcome one."

"It's still fruz," said old Hedgehog, emptying the milk on the table. "My wife sez to me, 'Miss Squirrel had a fine green bow on her tail at the skating,' and I sez to her, 'Maybe she'll be having company when she gets home and want a drop more milk' – or should say, seeing as it's fruz, a bit more milk."

"Come along, Hedgehog, and join the party," they cried, and he sat down on the settle, keeping his prickles to himself.

"Squirrel did have company, you were quite right," laughed Hare, "and she tied a bow on his tail too!"

After supper they sang the songs which animals love – "Hare went mowing the Barley," and "The Jolly Hedgehog," "Squirrel went gathering Nuts in May," and "He was a Water-rat." They ended up with "He's a jolly good fellow," and toasted Mole and Water-rat in a bottle of Primrose wine which the Rat had overlooked.

"Old friends to meet, old wine to drink, and old wood to burn," said Mole, holding high his glass, and then he and the Water-rat said good-bye, and walked along the quiet field paths to their homes.

The End of the Story

The Knot
Squirrel Tied

One morning Rat came to his house door and gazed up and down with a weary eye. Then he slowly hobbled out to the hazel spinney and made a crutch to help himself along.

Mrs. Rat shut the door after him, and sighed as she rocked the wicker cradle in which her baby lay.

"Hush-a-bye," she sang in a high shrill voice.

> "Father Rat will bring thee an egg,
>   He'll either steal or borrow or beg."

"Alas!" she sighed. "It has never been the same since he stole the food from Grey Rabbit's house, and that *impident* Squirrel tied a knot in his tail. No one can untie it! Poor Rat! He has indeed suffered for his misdoings!"

The little Rat wailed even louder than ever, and his mother shook him till his teeth rattled like ivory bells.

31

"Hush-a-bye," she sang.

Rat crept along under the shadow of the wall. No longer could he scamper in a light-hearted way with his tail rippling behind him. Now it always dragged in the heavy knot which Squirrel had tied to remind him of his wickedness. The knot was always in the way. It got entangled in briars. No longer could he poach or thieve or hunt.

"Every day I get thinner and thinner, I never can get a really good dinner," Rat told his friends at the Cock and Bull Inn.

He thought of this as he sidled along by the wall. At last he reached the farm buildings, and he climbed up the narrow stair into the hen-house. He knew the Speckledy Hen had laid an egg, for he had heard her cackling triumphantly, boasting to all the world, in her silly way, of her cleverness.

Rat crept through the little door and went to the nests. In one lay the big brown egg, which had the golden yolk Rat loved so much. He tucked it under his body, but when he started downstairs the knot in his tail caught in the doorway, and he overbalanced. At that moment the Speckledy Hen looked up from the farmyard below. She saw her precious egg clutched in the arms of the stumbling Rat, and she set up such a screech that a farm man ran to the door.

"My egg! Oh! My dear egg!" she shrieked.

Rat struggled to get free, and dropped the egg. It

rolled down the stairway and spilt on the ground, and Rat rushed to safety followed by clods of earth and sticks and stones.

"So near, and yet so far," he groaned, as he rubbed his sore shins and rested in a hole in the wall.

He waited till the noise had died down, which was a long time, for the Speckledy Hen talked loudly about it all morning.

"Thinner and thinner and thinner," moaned Rat, as he buckled his belt more tightly and slouched round the corner.

He crept into the barn where a fine bag of meal stood in a corner.

Here was a lucky find! He gnawed a hole in the sack, and had just started to eat the sweet delicious grain, when in his excitement he moved clumsily, and the knot in his tail thumped on the boards.

Bang! Like a drum it sounded, and into the room came the farmyard cat, with her eyes gleaming, and her large mouth wide open.

What a race Rat had for the door! How his tail thumped behind him! He only just got safely away, with his coat torn, and his felt hat left behind in the cat's claws!

"That was a near squeak," said he to a friend, as he mopped his brow, but the other rat only laughed and ran away.

"There's no sympathy among thieves," grumbled

Rat. He pulled his belt still tighter, and sat down to think.

"Hedgehog is a kindly soul," said he to himself. "I'll have a talk with him at milking time. Once I gave him a poached egg for little Fuzzypeg. Alas! Never again shall I poach an egg, I fear, but I will remind him of my past goodness."

He waited all afternoon till Hedgehog came trotting across the field with his yoke across his shoulders, and the couple of milk pails jingling-jangling on the chains.

The Rat watched Hedgehog milk a cow and turn away with the warm milk frothing in his little pails. He licked his lips hungrily and then stepped softly after.

Old Hedgehog heard the thump of the tail, and exclaimed, without turning round, "Is that you, Rat? Keep away from my milk pails."

"Hedgehog, Mr. Hedgehog, Sir Hedgehog," said Rat humbly. "A word with you, Sir. A word in your ear, Sir."

Hedgehog put down the pails and waited.

"I'm getting very thin," said the Rat. "I never get anything to eat nowadays."

"Yes," said Hedgehog. "We have all been more comfortable lately."

"I'm as thin as a lath," Rat went on, wiping his eyes with a ragged handkerchief. "I'm nearly a skellington."

"What do you want me to do, Rat? I'll give you a drink of milk if you like."

The kindly Hedgehog held out a pail and Rat drank it all up with eager gulps.

Hedgehog looked cross. "Now you've been and done it!" he grumbled. "That was the milk for your own family, and for Grey Rabbit, and Hare and Squirrel. I shall have to go back to the cowshed, and the cow will be much annoyed."

"Please, kind Hedgehog," whined Rat, as the Hedgehog turned back to the cowhouse. "Do give me some advice. Everyone knows how wise you are."

"First time I've been called wise," said Hedgehog.

"How can I get the knot undone, Hedgehog?" asked Rat.

"Let me look at it," said the Hedgehog. "Let me see what I can do. My fingers are all thumbs, but I'll use my prickles."

Rat shivered. "Oh! Oh! Oh-oo-ooh!" he squealed, as the Hedgehog pulled and tugged at the knot with his spikes.

"I can't undo it, Rat. Clever fingers fastened it. Who was it, Rat?"

"It was Squirrel," said Rat. "Well, you'd better ask Squirrel to unfasten it," said Hedgehog.

"It's no use," said the Rat. "If I go near the little house at the end of the wood, they hear me coming, and they bolt the doors."

Hedgehog pondered. "Go and ask Mole's advice," said he. "Tell him I sent you. Once you gave my little

Fuzzypeg an egg. It was a bad one, it's true, but still, it was a present."

It was a weary road to Mole's house, with never a vestige of food to be seen in the fields. There were buttercups, but no butter, blackberry-flowers, but no blackberries.

"How I wish I had never gone to Grey Rabbit's larder," said the Rat, as he tramped up the field and crawled under the gate.

There was Mole's house, with Mole digging up pignuts in his garden.

As Rat walked up to the door, Mole put down his spade, rubbed his hands on his handkerchief, and then looked round to see if any of his valuables were lying about. One could never be too careful with Rat.

"Good afternoon, Rat," said he. "May I ask what brings you here?"

"Please, Mole, can you untie the knot in my tail?" asked the Rat, in a tiny, sad little voice. "Hedgehog sent me to you."

Without a word Mole trotted indoors, and returned with a bowl of soup and a slice of bread.

"Eat this," said he. "Then I will look at the knot."

Rat thanked him and gobbled up the food. Then Mole seized the knot with his long pink fingers and struggled and tugged, but still the knot wouldn't come undone.

"It's Squirrel's tying," said he, "but I don't think even her clever fingers could undo this knot. The only one who can help you is Wise Owl."

"I daren't go to him," said Rat shortly. "I'm scared of him. A thin rat would be nothing to a hungry owl."

"Nothing venture, nothing win," replied Mole. "Take him a present, Rat, something special."

"I haven't got a present," said Rat to himself. "I am so poor, I have nothing." He put his hand in his pocket and brought out the ragged handkerchief and a bone. He looked at the bone for a few minutes and then laughed softly.

"I haven't even a knife, but my teeth are sharp, as sharp as a razor. They will do the job."

He sat down on a log and gnawed at the bone. He bit a piece off here, and a slip off there, and a snippet from one end, and a whiff from the other, working away, polishing, and rubbing as he went. He was so much interested in his work that night came before he had finished, and he took home his carving.

"Have you brought any food, Rat?" asked his wife, when she opened the door. "We've had nothing but vegetable soup to-day, and the milk, which came very late."

"Nothing, wife," said Rat, "but to-morrow I'm going to see Wise Owl. I've hopes, my dear, hopes!"

He showed his wife his bone and she sat admiring it as he continued his work. Even the baby Rat stopped crying and began to laugh when he saw what his father was making.

It was a white little ship with rigging and sails, and tiny portholes. There was a figurehead at the prow, a seagull with outstretched wings.

"How did you think of it?" asked the admiring Mrs. Rat. "I never knew you were so clever, Rat."

"Desperation!" said Rat grimly. "I saw ships a-sailing, long ago. When I was young I went for a voyage in one, but the food wasn't good, and I gave up that wandering life."

"Has it got a name, your white ship?" asked Mrs. Rat.

"I think I'd better call it 'The Good Hope,'" replied Rat.

The next day Rat set off with his finished ship in his pocket, and a clean handkerchief. It had taken him all morning to complete his work, but he had added some delicate carving to the sides. The billowing sails were nearly transparent with his polishing, and the ropes were like cobwebs. He forgot his hunger as he worked, and quite enjoyed himself.

"Work isn't such a bad thing," he told his wife. "I've never done any before." He whistled a cheerful tune.

On his way to Wise Owl's wood he had to pass little Grey Rabbit's cottage. Delicious smells came from the window, and Rat crept up to see what was being cooked. He didn't want to get to Owl's house till dusk, so there was plenty of time, and perhaps he might pick up a morsel of food, if he was careful.

Little Grey Rabbit and Squirrel were making tartlets.

Grey Rabbit rolled out the pastry with her little rolling-pin, and Squirrel lined the patty-pans ready for the raspberry jam.

"Grey Rabbit, Grey Rabbit," called Hare, running up the garden path and bursting into the kitchen. Rat hid under the juniper bush in the shadow, and Hare passed him without noticing.

"Grey Rabbit and Squirrel," said he. "Haymaking has begun. Daisy Field is cut. Can we all go and play in the hayfield? The grass will be hay by to-morrow with this sunshine."

"Oh, let's," cried Grey Rabbit, and she waved her rolling-pin excitedly. "We'll go when the men have gone home to-morrow evening."

"I know a corner where we can make hay all by ourselves, with no frogs and field-mice to bother us," said Squirrel, absent-mindedly putting the jam into her own mouth instead of into the patty-pans.

"We'll invite Mole and Hedgehog and Fuzzypeg to join us," said little Grey Rabbit, "and we'll have tea in the hayfield."

"I'll make some treacle toffee to take with us," said Hare. He took a saucepan and measured out butter and treacle and sugar. He stirred it over the fire, getting in Squirrel's way, and knocking over the flour bin. Then he ran to the garden for a pinch of lavender and sweetbriar and lad's-love, to give it a flavour. Rat held his breath. It was lucky he was as thin as a shadow, or Hare would

41

have seen him.

"That isn't treacle toffee!" exclaimed Squirrel indignantly.

"No, I've changed its name," said Hare, grinning. "It's Lavender Toffee." He stirred in his herbs, and the sweet smell came into the room.

Little Grey Rabbit put her tartlets in the oven, and Hare set his toffee on the window-sill to cool. Then they all went out in the garden and sat among the flowers, sipping lemonade, and fanning themselves with the leaves of the sycamore-tree.

Rat crept up to the back door, and looked into the cosy kitchen. He knew his way about quite well.

"Ah!" he sighed, and he dragged his unwilling tail over the doorway. "I'm safe for a few minutes," said he.

He crouched down by the fire, and sniffed the savoury smells of raspberry tartlets which came from the oven. He opened the oven door and poked his nose in the hot jam.

"Oh!" he squeaked in a muffled voice. "Too hot!"

He dipped the tip of his tail in the cooling toffee, but that was too hot, also. He squirmed round and looked at the burn. The knot seemed tighter than ever.

Through the open window he heard the three friends make plans for the picnic.

"There's my chance," said Rat. "I'll come along to-morrow and see what I can find. Now I'll go and have a word with Wise Owl."

He looked again at his little ship, white as ivory, and pretty as a picture. Then he shuffled out of the house, and went through the wood to Wise Owl's house in the great beech-tree. He rang the little silver bell which hung from the door, and the sleepy bird came to see who wanted him in the daylight.

Rat waved his handkerchief, and the Owl made a truce. "Rat!" said he gruffly. "What do you want?"

"I've brought you a present, Wise Owl." Rat spoke in a trembling voice.

Wise Owl sat waiting, with his large round eyes staring at the unfortunate rat, whilst Rat fumbled in his pocket and brought out the little ship.

"Hm-m," said Wise Owl, flying down and examining it. "A nice bit of carving. Pity you don't do more work, Rat. Why not try to work instead of to thieve?"

"Please, Wise Owl, will you unknot my tail?" asked Rat, holding up his paws in a supplicating way. "I am as thin as a leaf, and no one is clever enough to unknot me."

Owl hummed to himself, and turned the tiny bone ship over and over.

"I'm afraid you are still a thief, Rat. What about Speckledy Hen's egg?

"What about the farmer's corn? Where did that jam come from, which I see on your nose? And the treacle toffee on the end of your tail?"

Rat fidgeted uneasily. What keen eyes had Owl!

"The knot will stay tied until you turn over a new leaf,

Rat. No one can unfasten it. Turn over a new leaf!"

Owl shut his door and went back to his library, holding the little ship in his claws. He took down his book on sailing-ships, and examined the rigging.

"Quite correct in every detail," said he.

Rat hobbled painfully back through the wood, turning all the green leaves he could reach, but still his tail remained knotted. However, he felt happier, for he had made something, and Owl had looked pleased with it.

The next day, as usual, he paid his visit to the farmyard, to see what he could pilfer. He walked up to the hen-roost and there was the Speckledy Hen's latest egg. Rat looked at it with longing eyes. Speckledy Hen was a good-natured silly creature. He would leave her egg. There would be raspberry tartlets at Grey Rabbit's house.

He turned away and started to go down the stair.

Was it imagination? He felt a loosening in his tail. The knot thumped less noisily as he slid down.

"Cluck! Cluck!" cried the Speckledy Hen when she saw him. "Shoo, Rat! Shoo! Have you eaten my egg to-day as you are not carrying it?" She ran shrieking to her precious egg. There it was, safe and sound! She couldn't understand, and she clucked softly to herself, "Did Rat forget it, or has he turned over a new leaf?"

Rat went into the barn. There was a litter on the floor, and he seized a bunch of twigs and swept it away. Up and down the stones he went, sweeping softly, with scarcely a glance at the meal bag, until the floor was clean. Then he went up to the sack and gazed at its bulging sides.

A pity to mess up the floor again! There would be raspberry tartlets waiting for him. He turned away, and another little hitch in his tail seemed to be loosened.

He went to Hedgehog's house under the hedge.

"Can I do any little thing for you, Hedgehog?" he asked.

Old Hedgehog stared. "Do you mean a little burglary?" he asked.

"No. I'll help to carry your milk pails to the neighbours," said Rat.

"And drink the milk, like you did yesterday," replied the Hedgehog indignantly.

"Try me," said Rat, so Hedgehog trusted him with the milk for the Red Squirrel who lived up in the pine-tree. Hedgehog never liked taking milk to the Red Squirrel, who was so full of jokes, the staid old milkman didn't know what to make of him.

"'Twill give him a fright," thought Hedgehog. "Then maybe he'll be more polite to me. Once he sent an old-laid egg to Fuzzypeg!"

So Rat took the milk to the Red Squirrel's door, and knocked gently. He filled the jug at the foot of the tree, and turned away.

"Oh!" shouted the Red Squirrel. "A Rat! A Rat!" He fled to the top of his tree, and sat there peeping down.

When Rat was out of sight he crept down again, and looked around. His pyjamas, hanging on the clothes-line, were still there; his bowl of nuts was untouched; the milk-jug was filled to the brim!

Rat walked through the fields.

Both his heart and his tail felt lighter, and when he got back to Hedgehog's house, there was a mug of milk and a hunch of bread and cheese, waiting for him on the doorstep.

Fuzzypeg peeped round the corner, all ready to run away. Rat put his hand in his pocket and brought out a dozen oak-apples, which he gave to the astonished little hedgehog for marbles.

As evening came there were sounds of gaiety in the hayfield. In the far corner Squirrel and little Grey Rabbit in blue sun-bonnets were raking the hay, and Hare was piling it up into haycocks. Hedgehog and Fuzzypeg came to help and tossed it with their prickles. Then Mole joined them, with a little hayfork which he had made.

Rat stood looking at the happy scene – an outsider who mustn't venture near. He was on his way to Grey Rabbit's house, where he hoped to find the raspberry tartlets waiting for him. He wouldn't be caught this time! He knew his way about, and Squirrel was safe for an hour or two.

Then he noticed the feast spread out under the hedge, not far from him. There it lay, in the shade of the foxgloves, with no one to guard it! There was a little white cloth and on it a basket filled with the tempting raspberry tartlets! So it was of no use to go to the house, for the food was here!

There were nut leaves laden with wild strawberries and raspberries, and a jug full of cream. There was crab-apple jelly, and sloe jam, little green lettuces, and radishes like rose-buds, and a big plum cake, and the treacle toffee!

Rat's mouth watered. He stared so hard at the plum cake that he felt he could taste its delicious sugary crust. Then he turned away and walked home.

A great pink cloud like a bunch of roses lay in the sky, and swifts cut across the blue air. Rat gazed up at the birds, so light and free, and at that moment he felt light and free, too.

The last knot in his tail had come undone. He was a happy rat, loosened from his fetters, and he ran home to tell his wife, whisking his tail like a whip around his head.

"I saw Rat staring at our feast," confided Grey Rabbit to the others as they sat round in a circle among the foxgloves. "He didn't touch a thing, and he didn't know that I saw him."

"He was reminded of his past wickedness by the knot in his tail," said Squirrel, as she munched the nuts and strawberries; "and I tied that knot. It will never, never come undone."

"Rat helped to carry my milk to-day, and when I

went to the barn he had swept it clean," said old Hedgehog.

"Rat gave me some marbles," cried little Fuzzypeg.

"He seems a changed animal," said little Grey Rabbit.

"I wonder if Wise Owl gave him some good advice," mused the Mole.

The next morning Rat came to little Grey Rabbit's house. He carried a pair of shears and a scythe instead of his club and gun. He was neat and tidy, and he walked with a quick light step.

"Can I gather your firewood, Grey Rabbit?" said he. "Can I mow your lawn, or cut your hedge, or weed your garden?"

"Why! The knot has gone from your tail, Rat!" exclaimed Grey Rabbit. "Who untied it, Rat?"

"No one," replied Rat modestly. "It came undone by itself. I'm not a thief any more. I understand now what Wise Owl meant when he told me to turn over a new leaf. I shall work for my living, little Grey Rabbit."

He took up his shears and cut the hedge, making peacocks and balls and ships. He mowed the lawn smooth as silk.

He went in the wood to gather sticks, and as he passed under Owl's tree, the wise bird looked out.

"Ho! Ho!" he hooted. "A reformed Rat. The knot is not! A skilful Rat! An artist! Go on with the good work, Rat, and bring me another present someday. I shall be

honoured to accept it."

The Rat blushed through his dusky skin with pride, but he went on gathering sticks. When he had a great bundle he carried it to the door of the little house. At night he went home with his wages in his pocket, a respectable working animal.

"I'm going to carve something else," said he to his wife. "You've never seen anything like what I'm going to make!" He sat down at the table with his little white bone, and began to carve – but that is a secret for another time!

The End of the Story

Little Grey Rabbit
Makes Lace

Grey Rabbit sat at her cottage door one fine morning
with her work-basket at her side and the scissors on the
doorstep. She was making a night-cap for Mrs. Hedgehog out of a little pink handkerchief. Hare had picked
it up on the common, dropped from somebody's pocket.
Grey Rabbit decided it was just right for a night-cap.
She snipped the edge neatly and sewed a hem, shaping it
to fit Mrs. Hedgehog's head. Her little needle flew in and
out of the linen and her stitches were so small they were
almost invisible.

"This will keep Mrs. Hedgehog warm at night when
she peeps through the window at the moon," thought the
busy rabbit. "She got a cold, moon-gazing last month,
poor Mrs. Hedgehog. It was clever of Hare to find this
piece of linen. He is really a remarkable Hare."

It was very quiet in the cottage, for Hare and Squirrel

had gone out together across the fields to visit the Speckledy Hen, but in the trees all the birds were singing. Grey Rabbit could hear a blackbird playing his little flute, and a tom-tit ringing a peal of bells. A speckled thrush was calling.

"I see you. I see you. Kiss me. Kiss me." And a green woodpecker laughed loudly.

There was a flutter of wings and Robin the postman flew down with his letter-bag, from which he took a little green-leaf letter.

"You're lucky to-day, Grey Rabbit. Here's a letter."

"A letter for me?" cried Grey Rabbit, dropping her sewing.

"It's not very important. I read it first," said the Robin. "I should have come at once if it had been URGENT but it's nothing much. So I stopped to weed my garden first."

"Dear Robin," laughed Grey Rabbit. "I can't even read it, it has such crooked letters."

"It says: 'Riddle-me-ree, I'm coming to tea,'" said the postman. "Never a please or thank you, or anything."

"Who sent it?" asked Grey Rabbit, turning it over and looking at the back. Then she saw the letter F scribbled on the stalk.

"Ah! It's from Fuzzypeg," she cried. "He knows he is always welcome."

I might have guessed! I saw the little hedgehog go past with his schoolbag early this morning. I'll say good-bye, now, Grey Rabbit, and go back to my garden."

The Robin flew away with his empty postbag flapping behind him, and Grey Rabbit took up her sewing. The needle had fallen out, and she hunted in the grass for it.

"Cuckoo! Cuckoo!" cried a small squeaky voice, and there stood Fuzzypeg with his pointed nose pushed between the bars of the gate.

"Cuckoo! Did you think it was the Cuckoo, Grey Rabbit?" he asked, hopefully.

"Well, a prickly cuckoo with no wings," said Grey Rabbit, running to let him in. "Come along, little Fuzzypeg. I've just had a nice letter from you. I am so glad you've come."

"I thought I would and I did," said Fuzzypeg. "It was a holiday, and I didn't know, so I've been finding presents all day."

He slipped his paw in his left pocket and brought out a robin's pin-cushion. "It's the reddest pin-cushion I've ever seen on a rose-bush. It's for you to stick your pins in, Grey Rabbit."

Little Grey Rabbit thanked him and put it in her work-basket, but Fuzzypeg dived deep into his right pocket and brought out a double-daisy. Then he went to his left pocket for a peacock butterfly, and to his right for a ladybird in a spotted cloak. Finally from the left pocket came a green shining beetle.

"Oh, thank you, Fuzzypeg," said Grey Rabbit, as all these things appeared. The butterfly flew on the work-box and sunned its wings. The ladybird settled on the pink linen cap. The little emerald beetle walked straight to the needle and stood by it.

"Oh, look! He's found my lost needle," cried Grey Rabbit. "Isn't he clever!"

"I thought he was a special beetle," agreed Fuzzypeg. "That's why I brought him to see you."

He ran indoors and fetched a stool and sat down by his friend's side. He watched Grey Rabbit thread her needle and make her tiny stitches.

"What are you making, Grey Rabbit?" he asked.

"Hush! It's for your mother," she whispered. "It's a night-cap."

"She *will* be pleased, Grey Rabbit." Fuzzypeg stroked the soft linen admiringly. "She made a wish for a night-cap."

"Grey Rabbit," he continued, "I've seen something to-day."

"Yes? What is it?" Grey Rabbit smiled at the eager face turned towards her.

"I went across the common early this morning, to post your letter, and do you know, there was lace hanging on the gorse."

"Lace? What kind of lace?"

"Very nice lace, silver and grey, all dangling from the prickles. Where did it come from, Grey Rabbit?"

"I expect it was the spiders' weaving. They are clever creatures, Fuzzypeg. They hang out their silver webs in

the bushes to catch sunbeams."

"I tried to bring you some, but it all curled up to nothing," said Fuzzypeg.

"You can't carry it, Fuzzypeg dear."

"I think my mother would like some lace on her cap. Can you make it, Grey Rabbit? You can do most things," said the little Hedgehog.

"I can't make lace," sighed Grey Rabbit. "I'll ask Squirrel when she comes home. I can hear voices in the fields now. Squirrel and Hare will soon be here."

"Riddle-me-ree, I want my tea," sang Fuzzypeg, leaping up, and he and Grey Rabbit ran indoors to set the table.

Fuzzypeg toasted the muffins, and Grey Rabbit washed the lettuces and radishes, and put them on the little plates. She brought a cake from the larder and a loaf of currant bread from the bread-mug. There was a pat of butter, a jug of milk and a bowl of nuts. She was just making the tea when the garden gate rattled and Squirrel and Hare came racing up the path into the house. Fuzzypeg hid under the table. He suddenly felt shy.

"Is tea ready, Grey Rabbit? We are hungry!" cried Squirrel, tossing a bunch of flowers on the table.

"Grey Rabbit! Grey Rabbit!" shouted Hare. "We saw Speckledy Hen and she sent two eggs for your tea. I rolled one down a hill, and it went so fast I couldn't catch it."

"Not till it was broken," explained Squirrel. "Then we caught it, after it had bounced."

"Then we licked it up," added Hare.

"And where's the other egg?" asked Grey Rabbit.

"Well, we tried to see if it could swim," said Hare.

"And did it?"

"No, it was drowned in the stream among the forget-me-nots. Poor little egg," said Hare sadly.

"Poor little egg," echoed Grey Rabbit, and a tiny whimper came from under the table, but just then Hare noticed the little pink cap lying neatly folded on the work-basket. He snatched it up and set it on his long ears. Then he danced around singing:

"A hunting-cap for me.
A hunting-cap for me.
I'll catch the wicked Fox
And put him in a box,
And serve him up for tea."

"No, it's for me," cried Squirrel, grabbing the cap from Hare and perching it on her own red head, singing:

"A hunting-cap for me.
A hunting-cap for me.
I'll catch the little Weasel,
And beat him with a Teazel,
And never set him free."

"It isn't for either of you," shrieked an indignant,

muffled voice, and Fuzzypeg scrambled out and pulled Squirrel's tail. "It's for my mother." He was half-crying.

"Hello, Fuzzypeg! What are you doing here?" cried Hare.

"I've come for tea, and it's a hunting-cap for my mother, it is," sobbed Fuzzypeg.

"It's a night-cap for Mrs. Hedgehog, made out of the handkerchief you found, Hare," explained Grey Rabbit. "It's to keep her warm when she looks at the new moon."

"My mother always makes a c-c-c-curtsey to-o th-the n-n-new m-m-moon and she gets a w-w-wish," sobbed Fuzzypeg. "She w-w-wished for a hunt-hunt-night-cap and th-this is it."

"Now come along and have tea, all of you," said Grey Rabbit. "Fuzzypeg must have the biggest muffin, and the slice of cake with cherries on the top."

"Dry your eyes, Fuzzypeg, and sit by me," she continued, and Fuzzypeg rubbed his face in his smock and sat close to Grey Rabbit.

"Squirrel, can you make lace?" asked Fuzzypeg suddenly cheerful, as he gobbled up his muffin.

"No, I can't, but I know where Queen Anne's Lace grows," answered Squirrel.

"Queen Anne's Lace? What's that?" Fuzzypeg stared at Squirrel.

"It's the foamy white flower that fills the hedgebanks and ditches, where you hide when anyone goes past," said Hare.

"Oh, yes. I know it. I've often hidden in it."

"I once made a boot-lace," said Hare. "It was a very good one, made from a green rush, and I threaded it through a boot. What do you want lace for, Fuzzypeg? Would a boot-lace do?"

"It's for my mother's night-cap, to go round the edge," said Fuzzypeg.

Grey Rabbit explained about the gossamer lace which hung on the hedges and gorse-bushes. They all shook their heads, saying nobody could make lace except the spiders and perhaps the field-mice. The mice had sharp teeth, they could surely make lace.

"I'll go to-morrow to visit the field-mice and the spiders, Fuzzypeg, and when I have some lace I will trim the cap ready for the new moon."

"Yes, and when my mother makes her wish, I'll pop it on her head. Won't she be surprised!" laughed Fuzzypeg, clapping his hands.

When tea was over and every scrap on the tiny plates had been eaten, Fuzzypeg ran home.

Grey Rabbit finished sewing the cap, and Squirrel tried it on again.

"It would be lovely with lace round the edge," said she, running to look at herself in the glass.

The next day Grey Rabbit knocked at the door of the little house where the field-mice lived. They invited her to come in, but the house was so small Grey Rabbit thought she would stick fast. Through the open door she could see washing before the fire and a basket of sewing on the table. They were always busy because there were so many children.

"Excuse me, Mrs. Mouse, can you make lace?" asked Grey Rabbit, looking at the frills and little garments hanging there. "You sew so neatly I hope you can make lace."

"Lace, Miss Grey Rabbit? Oh no! We always bite the edges of our frills to make them shaggy, but we cannot weave lace."

So Grey Rabbit went to the common to ask the spiders about it. They took no notice of her. They were spinning their silken webs and running in and out of the golden gorse flowers, and they had no time for the rabbit.

"I don't think anybody can make lace," said she. So the pink night-cap lay in the work-basket, and the moon grew larger and larger till it was full moon. Then it began to wane, and Grey Rabbit was afraid the new moon would appear like a thin horn in the sky, and Mrs. Hedgehog would have no lace on her cap to greet it.

One sunny day Hare was coming home from a journey, and he took a short cut through the village. It was a bold thing to do, but the children were safe at school, the dogs were asleep, the ducks were busy swimming in the pond, and the cats and babies were curled up in their cradles. Only the blacksmith was tinkling on his hammer and the cobbler was tapping at his shoes.

From the school-room came singing, and Hare listened as he passed the door. He could hear these words chanted by fifty little voices:

"Queen Anne, Queen Anne,
  She sat in the sun,
  Making of lace till the day was done.
  She made it green, she made it white,
  She made it of flowers and sunshine and light.
  She fastened it on a stalk so fine,
  She left it in the hedgerow to shine.
  Queen Anne's Lace. Queen Anne's Lace.
  You find it growing all over the place."

Hare, with ears a-cock and every sense alert, stepped lightly on tip-toe down the street, past the little warm, thatched houses, and the village church and the White Hart Inn. At the door of a pretty cottage, all among roses and lilies, sat an old lady, and there was something about her that made Hare stop still.

For one thing, she smiled at Hare, and her smile was so sweet that Hare felt flattered. He waggled his long ears and smiled back.

For another thing, she was sitting on a low chair in the porch, with a dark pillow on her lap, and her fingers were moving as swiftly as two darting birds. Hare had never seen human fingers like hers. He was filled with curiosity as he gazed. Little brown wooden bobbins, like toys, with glass beads dangling down, were flying to and

66

fro, and spidery threads were twisting as if a wind blew them.

"She is making music, playing a tune on the pillow," thought Hare, as he listened to the tinkle of the glass beads, and the murmur of the old lady's song as she worked.

"Queen Anne, Queen Anne,
    She sat in the sun,
    Making of lace till the day was done."

Then, "Good morning, Mr. Hare," she called, nodding her old head in its sun-bonnet, and tapping with her toes. Her fingers never stopped flying over the pillow, twisting the threads, and then moving some scarlet-headed pins.

"Good morning, Queen Anne," said Hare politely, remembering the manners Grey Rabbit had taught him, and he made a little stiff bow.

"Miss Susan," said the old lady. "That's my name."

"Good morning, Queen Anne," repeated Hare, bowing once more. "Please, what are you doing?"

"What do you think, Mr. Hare?" laughed Miss Susan, whose blue eyes twinkled like two stars.

"I think you are either playing a tune or making Queen Anne's Lace, like the flowers in the hedges," said Hare.

"Clever Hare! I am making lace," said Miss Susan, and her old fingers moved more quickly than ever as she tossed the bobbins about.

Hare leapt up to her, and quite startled her so that she nearly dropped the pillow and all.

"Oh, I am so glad to see you, Queen Anne," said he. "Grey Rabbit wants to make lace. How do you do it?"

"Please don't jump so wildly, Mr. Hare," said the old lady, as she settled herself again, and arranged the pillow and straightened the threads which hung from the bobbins. "You frightened me. Now watch how I do it."

Hare stood close to her on the door-step, with the lilies and roses waving near. A cart-horse walked slowly up the road, and a man followed towards the smithy where the blacksmith was working, but nobody saw Hare.

He stared at her nimble fingers, following the pattern pricked on a strip of paper laid on her lace-pillow. Every little wooden bobbin was cut in a charming shape, with red, blue and white beads dangling at the ends. The piece of lace with its lovely design lay there, ever growing longer before Hare's eyes.

As she worked the old lady talked to Hare, and told him about lace-making. He told her about Squirrel, Grey Rabbit, Wise Owl, and Moldy Warp, and the cap Grey Rabbit had made for Fuzzypeg's mother. She said it was the nicest tale she had heard for many a long day.

He would have been there all day if there hadn't been the tinkle-tinkle of a bell in the school-room, and the scamper of little feet in heavy boots, and the laughter of children pouring down the road, free from lessons. They gave a shout when they saw Hare standing by Miss Susan, but Hare saw them in time.

"Look! There's a Jack Hare! Catch him! Catch him and put him in a pot. Come on! After him! Let's cook him for dinner."

Hare ran for his life, with his ears laid flat and his big eyes starting with fright.

"Now, children, do 'ee be kind to all of God's creatures," said Miss Susan, dropping the lace-pillow and stepping into the road, but the children raced along and Hare flew in front of them. Dogs and cats, ducks and drakes, cobbler and blacksmith, all joined in the race.

"And I won! I won!" cried Hare breathlessly, as he dashed into the cottage and flung himself in the rocking-chair. "They ran and they ran, but the couldn't catch me. I'm the swiftest runner of all. Oh, I'm a wonderful Hare."

"Yes, of course, but where have you been, Hare?" asked Grey Rabbit, as she stooped over the panting animal and wiped his hot face.

"I've been watching Queen Anne make lace, and I can tell you all about it."

"Hare! Hare! Have you really discovered Queen Anne?" cried the delighted Squirrel, bringing Hare a drink of water.

"She lives in the village and she showed me how to make most beautiful lace. You want a pillow."

"There's a pillow on my bed," said Grey Rabbit,

scampering upstairs to fetch it.

"And you want bobbins," continued Hare. "Not cotton-reels, but long bobbins, all carved and made pretty with beads on the ends."

"I'll make them for you," said Rat, pushing his ugly face in at the open door. "I saw Mister Hare running for his life, and I came to help. I'll carve those bobbins for you."

"And I'll get the beads," squeaked Fuzzypeg, peering round after the Rat. "I saw you running, Hare. It was a race."

Hare frowned and continued his directions.

"You will want a paper pattern with flowers or something pricked on it," said he.

"We'll make the paper pattern, Grey Rabbit, with our sharp teeth. We just came to see why Mister Hare was running so fast."

Hare frowned again as the family of field-mice crowded in the doorway, and he alarmed them so much they retreated to the garden.

"And you will want some fine long threads to make the lace," said he gruffly.

"There is plenty of sheep's wool in the hedges," Squirrel cried. "I use it for my knitting, and I can twist fine threads with it."

So the Rat made the lace-bobbins, carved in lovely shapes, some from pieces of bone and some from wood. Fuzzypeg hung beads of hawthorn and berries at the ends for weights.

The field-mice made lace patterns, pricking the paper with rows of bees and flowers. Squirrel wound the wool thread on the bobbins and Hare collected sharp-pointed thorns from the hedges for the lace-pins.

Then everybody (except Mrs. Hedgehog, who couldn't understand why the animals were so secretly busy) came to see Grey Rabbit make lace.

The little Rabbit sat at the door with her pillow on her knee, and the bobbins hanging down. She tossed the bobbins over and crossed the threads and moved the pins down the paper pattern, while they all watched her paws. A tiny strip of lace appeared, and it took the shape of a bee. On she went, and a flower came, and then another bee. She made a row of bees and flowers, with a wavy edge to the sheep's-wool lace like flowing water.

The mice squeaked in excitement, and Fuzzypeg danced with joy. Hare rushed out to find more wool for Squirrel to twist for the thread, and Rat carved another bobbin.

Grey Rabbit's paws, which had moved slowly at first, now flashed backward and forward, and the piece of lace hung down like gossamer.

"I can hold it," cried Fuzzypeg. "It doesn't melt away like the spiders' lace."

Then Grey Rabbit sewed it round the night-cap for Mrs. Hedgehog, just in time for the rising of the new moon.

Mrs. Hedgehog went outside to see the moon. She stood in the chilly evening light, and when she saw the lovely pale sickle of the moon in the sky, she solemnly bowed three times. Fuzzypeg, standing by her side, bowed too.

"I wish for a night-cap to keep my head warm," murmured Mrs. Hedgehog.

"I wish for some lace round your night-cap," said Fuzzypeg.

Then, from behind his back, he brought out the pink linen night-cap with sheep's-wool lace edging it, and a ribbon bow which Squirrel had kindly provided. He popped it on his mother's head, and how delighted she was!

"I have never seen such a lovely cap in all my born days," cried Mrs. Hedgehog, hugging Fuzzypeg. "Real lace, with bees and flowers all round the edge. It must have been made by a Fairy."

So that is how Grey Rabbit made lace. She trimmed a petticoat for Squirrel and made a cravat for Water-Rat. All the baby rabbits had lace caps. Even Wise Owl got a piece of lace for a keepsake, but he ate it, thinking it was bread and butter.

In the village Miss Susan told a strange story.

"Do you mean to tell us that a Hare came to watch your lace-making?" asked the neighbours.

"He did indeed, and he was a very intelligent Hare. He called me Queen Anne," said Miss Susan proudly.

"Then he can't have been intelligent, because everyone knows Queen Anne is dead," they scoffed. "You must have dreamed it!"

"You fell asleep and a Hare came past, and all the children ran after him."

"I wasn't asleep," protested Miss Susan. "He asked about lace-making and I showed him how to do it."

Nobody believed Miss Susan, but Robin the postman, who was sitting on a spade handle, heard this, and he told Hare.

"We'll hang a piece of lace on Queen Anne's door-knob. Then she can show the village," said Hare.

Grey Rabbit made the most beautiful strip of lace, and Robin the postman hung it on the door-knob of the thatched cottage.

"Now look!" cried the old lady triumphantly, showing it to her neighbours. "This isn't my work. Did you ever see such lace as this? Grey Rabbit must have made it and Hare told her how to do it and I told Hare."

"We'll put it in the village museum," they said. "It's the strangest lace ever known, and as fine as a fairy's work."

There it lies, in a glass case, with a Queen Elizabeth shilling and a stone arrow-head. People stare at its beauty, and wonder who made it, but we know, don't we?

"Sing the song again, Grey Rabbit, the song Hare told you," pleaded Fuzzypeg. "My mother wants to hear it."

"Yes, please sing it, Grey Rabbit," said Mrs. Hedgehog. She wore her night-cap in the day as well as at night, she liked it so much.

So Grey Rabbit sang the little song and they all joined in the chorus:

"Queen Anne, Queen Anne, she sat in the sun,
Making of lace till the day was done.
She made it green, she made it white,
She made it of flowers and sunshine and light.
She fastened it to a stalk so fine,
She left it in the hedgerow to shine.
Queen Anne's Lace. Queen Anne's Lace.
You find it growing all over the place."

The End of the Story

Little Grey Rabbit's May Day

The wild winds of March had died away. April had come with sweet-tasting rain and tender grasses and the Cuckoo's call. Now May was near and every little creature rejoices when it is Maytime.

"It's May Day tomorrow," announced Hare at breakfast time one morning. "There's going to be dancing round the Maypole in the village. The Maypole is set up ready with fine ribbons hanging down and the children will dance like me."

"How do you know?" asked Squirrel, calmly eating her nuts. "You can't dance round the Maypole, Hare."

"Well, you're wrong, Squirrel," retorted Hare. "I danced round last night when the children had gone to bed, so there!"

"Hare! did you? In the moonlight?" cried Grey Rabbit, astonished.

"Yes, all alone by the light of the moon," laughed Hare. "I tried to bring you a ribbon but they were fastened out of my reach. I jigged till I heard the policeman's heavy tread and then I scampered away."

"So that is why you were so late," sighed Grey Rabbit.

"Could we have a Maypole, Grey Rabbit?" asked Squirrel. "I want to dance round it and I'm afraid to go to the village."

"We'll dance round the May tree and that's better than a Maypole," said Grey Rabbit. "There's a lovely May tree in the field with blossom coming out already."

"Let's have a procession like the children in the village," said Hare, leaping up with excitement. "The Pussycat told me about it. They sing a carol and carry crowns and sceptres."

"Let me think," implored Grey Rabbit. "Let me think." And she put her paw to her head and stood very still.

"I'll think too," said Squirrel, imitating her and standing very still, too.

"I can think without this fuss," said Hare, scornfully, and he drank his mug of milk.

"We must gather lots of flowers early on May morning," said Grey Rabbit. "We must pick them with May-dew on their petals. I'll take a jug to catch some May-dew, for it's magical. We must make crowns and garlands for May."

"Who is May?" asked Squirrel.

"May is the spirit of Spring," said Grey Rabbit. "I think I must ask Wise Owl about all this."

So away they went after the breakfast things were washed to find Wise Owl.

On the way Hedgehog and Moldy Warp joined them.

"May Day?" asked Wise Owl, sleepily, looking down at the company. "How to keep May Day? You ought to know. May is the Queen of the flowers. You must make crowns and sceptres for her. She's invisible, but you hang them on a May tree and she will find them."

"Yes, crowns and sceptres for the Queen," echoed Grey Rabbit, and all the rest stared at Wise Owl.

"It's in my Book of Wisdom," went on the great bird. He went back to the little room in his tree and brought out the green book which contained so much knowledge of birds and animals. "On May Day make a crown of flowers and a sceptre and cowslip balls. Take them to a May tree," he read slowly, spectacles on beak.

"What kind of flowers, Wise Owl?" called Hare.

"It doesn't say," answered Wise Owl and he turned a page. "Oh, yes, it says 'Cowslips and all Spring flowers but at the top of the crown there must be a Crown Imperial.'"

"I've never heard of a Crown Imperial." "What is it?" "Does it grow in the woods?" "Is it wild or tame?" They all talked at once.

Wise Owl shook his head, but Moldy Warp spoke up.

"I once saw a fine flower in the garden of the Big

House," said he. "I saw the Crown Imperial. I heard the head-gardener tell the under-gardeners there was a pearl in each lily bell, like a tear. I didn't stop long for they set mole-traps when they see my nice mole-hills."

"What was it like?" asked Grey Rabbit.

"It was like a ring of golden bells with a green topknot of leaves," said the Mole. "I sat underneath it."

"Then I've seen it in the village," said Old Hedgehog slowly. "Sometimes there are orange bells, Mr. Moldy Warp."

Moldy Warp frowned. "The Crown Imperial is a noble lily and it lives in grand gardens," said he.

"In cottage gardens, too," said Hedgehog. "I've seen it in Miss Susan's border."

Hare leapt up. He sprang so high that Wise Owl shook his head at him and ruffled his feathers.

"I've seen it too," he shouted. So Wise Owl turned his back and returned to the tree.

"Noisy crowd, always argy-bargying," he murmured. "I won't read to them."

"It grows in Queen Anne's border," cried Hare. "Miss Susan taught me to make lace. I was looking out of the corner of my eye and I saw a tall yellow lily."

"You'd better get one from the Old Lady," said Hedgehog.

"Yes, I will," said Hare.

"What can I do?" asked Fuzzypeg, who joined his father on the way home.

"You can make cowslip balls, Fuzzypeg. You know where cowslips grow, and you are a good ball-maker," said Grey Rabbit.

"Let me make a sceptre," called little voices from all over the place, as heads popped from holes and tree trunks and rocky shelters.

"Yes, all of you can make sceptres on May morning," said Grey Rabbit and they hurried back home.

On May morning, as soon as the bright sun peeped from the horizon and the birds were singing their May Day hymn, a company of small animals came from their cottages and ran to the fields and hedgebanks to gather fresh flowers with dew on the petals. Grey Rabbit carried a tiny jug for May-dew and Squirrel had a basket for flowers, but Hare was impatient to discover the Crown Imperials in the village street.

Then Moldy Warp shut his door and stepped across the dewy field, every now and then stopping to pick a few cowslips and wild purple orchis. The wind was playing in the trees like a little barrel-organ, and the beech leaves waved up and down like swing-boats at a fair.

Moldy Warp went to a willow by the stream and began to cut withies with his little axe. Then Grey Rabbit, Squirrel and Hare came up.

"A happy May Day," they called. "Why are you getting withies?" they asked.

"Why? Because you must have a foundation for the crowns and garlands you clever ones are going to make,"

84

said he, scornfully, and he stripped off the tender leaves and twined the slender withies to make hoops and rings.

"You fasten the flowers to these," he explained. "You didn't listen to Wise Owl last night but he would have told you."

"I'm going to the village to get the Crown Imperials from Queen Anne's garden," said Hare, as he impatiently twisted the willow and tied a few bunches of flowers to the framework.

"You can't just go and take Miss Susan's precious flowers without asking," objected Grey Rabbit.

"Give her a cowslip ball," suggested Squirrel.

Little Fuzzypeg was sitting near them with a basket of cowslips. He was so busy threading the golden heads on a string of plaited grasses he could not bother to watch Moldy Warp. By his side lay two beautiful cowslip balls, even and round.

"Can I have one for Miss Susan?" asked Grey Rabbit, stooping to admire his work. She picked up a ball and smelled its honey scent and tossed it and caught it.

"Yes, Grey Rabbit dear," said the little Hedgehog. "I like Miss Susan. She is kind to little animals."

"I've got a hanky made of cobweb," said Grey Rabbit, putting her paw in her pocket. "I'll send that too."

"I've got a walnut shell with nothing in it," said Squirrel, and she held out an empty shell.

"Fill it with new-mown hay," said Grey Rabbit. So

Squirrel picked some of the white starry flowers of wood-ruff, which have the smell of fresh hay, and filled the little box. She tied the walnut's lid with green grasses, and it made a scent-box for Miss Susan.

"I've got something at home for the Old Lady," said Moldy Warp. "I'll go back to my cupboard where I keep my bits and bobs of findings. I've cut enough withies for you now."

Hare scampered along by the side of the slow-plodding Mole.

"Not much time to waste," said he as he leapt round his friend, urging him on. "I must get those Crown Imperials before even the blacksmith wakes up. Nobody must see me."

"Take your time, Hare. Go and pick flowers for the garlands. I can't hurry any faster. I won't be long," said Mole.

Moldy Warp unlocked his door and disappeared in his dark house. He went to the cupboard in the earthy wall. Some of Badger's findings from deep underground were there, and his own ancestral collection of treasures.

"I could give her an arrow-head," he pondered, stroking a grey stone, "or a Roman penny, or this bone pin carved with a hare at the end, or a jet ring – yet it might not fit her."

He turned over the little gold coins, the twisted gold wire, the flints and arrowheads and little stone lamps.

Then he pounced on something and took it to the

light. It was a tiny bottle only two inches long, green as grass, square and squat.

"This'll do. I'll fill it with dew from Grey Rabbit's jug, and it will make her young again. Yes, this'll do for Miss Susan or Queen Anne or whatever Hare calls her."

He hesitated a moment longer, and then he took the carved bone pin with the hare on top, and put it with the bottle. He tossed the rest of the things back in the cupboard, and went out to the impatient Hare.

"Hello, Moldy Warp. I thought you were going to stay all day," said Hare crossly. "What have you got? A dirty little green bottle and an old bone pin with me on the top?"

"Never you mind," said Moldy Warp, and he trotted back twice as fast, eager to show his finds to the company. He looked important as he drew his treasures out of his velvet pocket, and the animals left their crowns and sceptres to look.

"Here's a Roman bottle they kept their tears in," said he.

"I'm sure Queen Anne doesn't cry," protested Hare.

"We are going to put some of Grey Rabbit's May-dew into it," said Moldy Warp, glancing at Grey Rabbit's jug.

"Yes, I gathered it from the May-blossom as soon as the sun rays shone on it. It's magical," said Grey Rabbit.

"If Miss Susan puts a drop of this May-dew on her eyes she will see more clearly and need no spectacles," said Moldy Warp. "A drop on her cheeks will make the wrinkles vanish, and a drop on her crooked fingers will give her new strength."

So very carefully Moldy Warp filled the tiny green bottle from Grey Rabbit's jug of May-dew and Hare stuffed a wad of hawthorn in the top for a cork.

"Sorry I was cross, Moldy Warp," he muttered.

"That's all right," said Moldy Warp kindly as he held up the bone pin. "It's a Roman pin to fasten up her dress," said he.

"She can use it for a lace-bobbin," said Hare. "It's just like the bobbins that hung from her lace pillow. Thank you very much, Moldy Warp."

"Now go off, Hare, and take all these presents and the cowslip ball. Miss Susan will gladly give you a Crown Imperial," they told him, and away he galloped.

In his big pockets he carried the Roman bottle, the walnut shell filled with new-mown hay and the cobweb handkerchief. On his arm dangled the cowslip ball, sweet as honey.

But Hare was late. The children, too, had been up at dawn, putting the finishing touches on their crowns and sceptres.

Hare could see boys and girls having breakfast, while the garlands lay in the cool shadows outside, ready for the procession.

In every crown sat a little doll, and at the top of each crown was a fine Crown Imperial. Hare glanced at them uneasily.

"I hope they've left me one or two," he muttered as he dashed down the road towards Miss Susan's cottage.

Yes, there under the wall of the cottage was a row of fine golden flowers, each with five bells and a green topknot.

Miss Susan was proud of her tall lilies. Yellow brimstones flew among them and bumble-bees sipped the honey.

"Please, Miss Susan! Please, Queen Anne!" cried Hare, as he banged on the door with his furry fists. Nobody answered. Miss Susan was not well, her eyes were tired, her worn hands were weary.

"Miss Susan," called Hare, urgently, for he was afraid he had been seen as he ran through the village.

But Miss Susan lay in her bed, half-dreaming.

"A Happy May Day," squeaked Hare through the keyhole.

"Same to you," murmured Miss Susan. Then she started. "Who can it be? A mouse?" she asked herself. "Is it one of the children? Do they want some Crown Imperials for their May Day? Here I lie, and once I was Queen of the May. Now I can't even get up on May morning."

She listened, but there was no patter of feet, only a rustle as Hare slipped among the tall lilies.

"Who's there?" she called.

"It's only Hare. I want something," squeaked Hare,

but she could not hear his high voice. Hare cut two lilies, panting as he bit through the thick stalks, looking around nervously as footsteps came near.

"He went in here! He's gone somewhere about here!" said a boy's voice.

Hare hurriedly dropped his presents where the Crown Imperials had grown – the tiny Roman tear bottle filled with the dew of May, the Roman pin with a Hare on the top, the walnut shell stuffed with new-mown hay, the little lace handkerchief – but the cowslip ball he hung on the door knob. Then, clutching the golden flowers he leapt down the steps and away.

"After him! Catch him! A hare's been taking Miss Susan's lilies," the children cried as they tore after him. But nobody can catch a hare at full gallop, and Hare got safely away.

Later on the procession was formed. The children carried their heavy crowns on sticks threaded through the back of the flowery burdens. Auriculas and primulas, cowslips and bluebells covered the wicker frames, and at the tip of each crown and sceptre was a noble Crown Imperial. Inside the crown sat a small doll with a veil, for that is the old custom. The procession of children went from the school to the village green and they sang the May Day carol.

Miss Susan dressed slowly and looked out at the children as they passed her door with their crowns and garlands.

"Miss Susan, Miss Susan," they called. "There was a hare in your garden this morning, early. He took your Crown Imperials."

"Whatever did he want with my flowers?" wavered Miss Susan sadly, as she saw her broken lily stems.

"For his May dinner, I 'specks," laughed a little boy. "We nearly cotched him and made him into our dinner."

"I wish my flowers had gone to make a crown," said Miss Susan, and she turned away. Then she stopped for she saw the cowslip ball hanging on the door knob. Then something among the lily leaves caught her eye. She picked up the walnut and inside were the flowers of new-mown hay. She found the wee small handkerchief of cobweb and the bone carved pin with the hare on the top. She stooped down and picked up the little green bottle of ancient glass, with its stopper of hawthorn. She sniffed at it and poured a drop on her hands. "Nice smell," said she. She tasted it and rubbed a little on her aching head and eyes. Her headache vanished, and she could see the feathers of the birds, the petals of the flowers. Her eyes sparkled, her face was fresh and young again.

"This pin will make a lace-bobbin. Where did these things come from? Not from the school-children. This hanky is a fairy thing."

Then she remembered the children said a hare had been in the garden. A hare!

"Once I taught a hare to make lace. Yes, that's it. On

May Day anything might happen."

Away in the pasture another little procession was forming. Grey Rabbit fastened the Crown Imperial to the top of the lovely crown, which was made of cowslips, bluebells, king-cups and forget-me-nots.

"There was a doll in the crown I saw," said Hare.

"Yes, there ought to be a doll by rights," said Moldy Warp. "Who's got a doll?"

They looked at one another. "I haven't a doll," said Grey Rabbit. "Nor me. Nor me," said Squirrel and Fuzzypeg.

Then Rat stepped forward from behind a rock where he had been watching the scene.

"I can make a doll for you," said he. "I made one for our baby, out of a bit of bone. I can carve a doll all right."

He picked up a bit of oak and shaped it with his teeth so that there appeared a pretty little figure.

"How clever you are, Rat," said Grey Rabbit.

"Too clever by half," muttered Hare. Nobody had told him he was clever to get the Crown Imperials.

"Hush! That was rude," whispered Grey Rabbit, and she dressed the little doll in a skirt of leaves and made a bodice of cowslips. On its head she put a crown of May-blossom, and in its hand a bluebell wand.

So the flowery doll sat in the middle of the crown, under the great Crown Imperial.

Grey Rabbit and Squirrel slung the crown on a hazel

stick and carried it between them. Hare walked in front
with a tall Crown Imperial sceptre. Fuzzypeg followed
after with two cowslip balls. Then came Mr. Hedgehog
and Mrs. Hedgehog with a smaller crown of May-
blossom, and after them Water Rat carrying a water-lily
sceptre. Moldy Warp followed with a sceptre of crab-
apple blossom, and the little Hedgehogs, Bill and Tim,
walked with a garland of May and bluebells.

As they went their winding way to the old twisted
hawthorn, the animals sang their own May song. Their
tiny voices were mingled with those of the cuckoo
calling, the nightingale singing, the robins and wrens,
the blackbirds and throstles, all chanting with joy
because it was May Day.

"May, May, we sing to the May
To sun and moon and Milky Way,
To field and wood and growing hay,
On the First of May.

Grey Rabbit and Hare, Squirrel and all,
Fuzzypeg with his cowslip ball,
We carry the crown for beautiful May,
The sceptres and garlands,
This joyful day.
May Day. The First of May."

They hung the crowns and sceptres on the May tree,
and then they danced around. The May tree rustled her

branches and sent waves of perfume up to the blue sky, while all the birds came flying to the tree to join in the song of welcome to May.

At night, when everybody was fast asleep, Wise Owl flew over the May tree. The tree shone like silver, and in its branches hung the crown of flowers with the Crown Imperial, the sceptres and the cowslip balls.

"Too whit. Too whoo,
Happy May to you."

called Wise Owl; and then he listened, for he could hear a silvery answer which seemed to come from the tree itself.

"May Day. May Day. May Day," sang the tree and Wise Owl shivered with delight.

The End of the Story

97

Little Grey Rabbit's Birthday

Squirrel and Hare were gardening one fine day. Squirrel was sowing dandelions and Hare was watering them.

"It's little Grey Rabbit's birthday on Midsummer Day," said Squirrel, as she shook the dandelion clocks and let the seeds fly.

"I think it's time for my birthday," pondered Hare, idly swinging the watering-can. "It's weeks and weeks since I had a birthday. It's days and days. It's hours and hours ago."

"It isn't your turn, Hare. You are always having birthdays. Grey Rabbit hasn't had one for a whole year. We must give her a nice present," said Squirrel.

"Of course," agreed Hare quickly. "A very nice present. A cake or something. Yes, something we can all share."

"Yes, Hare. A birthday cake with candles on it," said Squirrel.

"I don't like the taste of candles," objected Hare. "Mice eat candles, not Hares."

"They are not to eat," cried Squirrel, laughing. "They are to show how old you are. Three candles if you are three years old."

"And a hundred if you are a hundred years old," said Hare. "Oh Squirrel, can we make the cake ourselves?"

"I think so," nodded Squirrel. "We can't ask Grey Rabbit to make it. It must be a secret."

Just then Grey Rabbit came running out of the house.

"Oh, Squirrel!" she cried. "I asked you to sow lettuce seed and you are putting dandelions in the garden. There's another gardener who will sow that for us."

"Who's that?" asked Squirrel.

"The wind. He will plant dandelion seeds, but he doesn't trouble over lettuce."

"The wind! I'm not friends with him. He blows too hard."

"Grey Rabbit!" interrupted Hare. "Squirrel and I have been saying that your b—b—— that it will be your b—b——"

"Hist! Never a word!" whispered Squirrel.

"No! Never a word! It's a secret," said Hare hastily.

"A secret from me?" asked Grey Rabbit, astonished.

"We can't tell you. It wouldn't be a secret if you knew," explained Squirrel.

"No, we can't speak it. It's something that must never be told," added Hare with importance.

Grey Rabbit stared at them. "Never?" she asked.

"Well," hesitated Squirrel, "not till – not till——" and she shut her mouth tightly lest the secret should escape.

But the secret was just about to hop out of Hare's mouth when Squirrel rushed at him with a handkerchief and tied him up.

"Have you got the toothache?" asked Grey Rabbit. "Poor Hare!"

Hare shook his head, but not a word could he utter.

"It's to keep the secret safe," confided Squirrel.

"You are a funny pair," laughed Grey Rabbit. "Will you come for a walk to visit the Speckledy Hen? I want some eggs for tea."

"Oh, we'll come, won't we, Hare?" said Squirrel, throwing down her rake.

"Mum-mum-mum-mum!" grunted Hare. He was wondering how he could eat an egg for tea with a handkerchief tied round his chin. He tried to ask Squirrel but he could only growl. There was nothing to be done but to follow Squirrel and Grey Rabbit.

They went through the field where Moldy Warp lived. Old Moldy Warp sat at the door of his house, smoking his pipe and sunning himself. On a tray by his side he had some clover and wild thyme drying in the sun, and every now and then he put a pinch in his pipe and smoked it.

"Hello!" he cried, rising as he saw the three little folk

coming over the grass. "This is a surprise!"

He hurried into his round house for some of the heather-ale which Badger had given him. He filled three glasses, the size of cob-nuts, and brought them to his friends.

"Oh dear! Have you got the toothache, Hare?" he asked.

"No. He's keeping a secret," explained Squirrel.

Hare looked at the heather-ale, and he looked at Squirrel. Then he began to tug at the handkerchief, till Mole took pity on him and untied the tight knot. Hare panted and puffed and drank the sweet honeyed wine.

"I'm going to tell," he exclaimed. "I can't keep it in. I shall burst if I tell nobody."

"No! No!" cried Squirrel, shaking his arm.

"Come inside and whisper to me and the doorpost," said Mole kindly. Hare followed him into the passage, and then he spoke up.

"It's Grey Rabbit's birthday on Midsummer Day, and we are going to make a cake," said Hare breathlessly.

"Ah! That is a good secret!" agreed Mole. "I'll give her a present."

"And come to tea with us," said Hare, "and taste the cake."

"Thank you Hare," said Mole. "I don't think I need tie you up again. You won't tell Grey Rabbit now you've told me and the doorpost."

Mole and Grey Rabbit talked about the summer flowers, the bees and the birds, and the three friends said good-bye. Grey Rabbit led the way through the edge of the wood. In the distance was the great beech tree that was Wise Owl's house. Hare looked at the silver bell, but he was afraid to pull it. Squirrel ran up the tree and called softly through the open window.

"Wise Owl! Wise Owl! It's Grey Rabbit's birthday on Midsummer Day."

"Gr-gr-gr," snored Wise Owl, but he heard in his dreams all the same.

They passed into the fields, where Milkman Hedgehog was coming back from the milking.

"Can we have a drink?" asked Squirrel, dancing up to him.

"It's thirsty work, keeping secrets," said Hare.

"We like new milk warm from the cow," said Grey Rabbit, and she twisted a leaf into a cup and held it out to him.

Hedgehog filled the leafy cup and they all sipped the milk, and laughed as they wiped the creamy moustaches from their lips.

Hare took old Hedgehog aside, and whispered to him:

"It's Grey Rabbit's birthday on Midsummer Day. We are going to make her a cake, and you can come and taste it."

"Ah! Thank ye!" cried Hedgehog. "I'll bring some milk to mix it. It'll make a tiddly present for Miss Grey

Rabbit."

"Mind, it's a secret," warned Hare.

"Mum's the word," said Hedgehog, and he touched his lips.

"Come along, Hare. We shall never get to the Speckledy Hen's house," called Grey Rabbit, "if you spend all the time telling secrets."

"Ha! Ha! Wouldn't you like to know?" teased Hare.

"Yes, I should," confessed Grey Rabbit.

"Well, dear Grey Rabbit, I will tell you," said Hare, and he went up to her. "I will whisper to you."

"Hare!" frowned Squirrel. "Do you want to be tied up again?" and Hare quickly sprang away.

When they arrived at the farm, there was the Speckledy Hen walking out with her little sunshade over her head.

"We've come for some eggs, Speckledy Hen," said Grey Rabbit. While the Hen was filling the basket, Hare went up to her and whispered in her tiny feathered ear.

"It's Grey Rabbit's birthday on Midsummer Day. We are going to make a cake, and you can come and taste it."

"I'll bring a present for dear Grey Rabbit," whispered the Hen. "And mind you put plenty of eggs in the cake, Hare. I will put a few extra ones in the hedge at the bottom of your garden."

The next day Squirrel and Hare decided to make the cake.

"We must get Grey Rabbit out of the way and do it secretly," said Hare. "Won't she be surprised! She doesn't know we can make cakes."

"We don't know either," muttered Squirrel. She was doubtful, but Hare was full of confidence.

"We must use cunning to send her away," continued Hare. "We must be wise as Wise Owl, clever as Moldy Warp and sensible as Water-rat, and lure her out of the house."

"All right. Do it," said Squirrel.

"Grey Rabbit! Grey Rabbit! Go away! We don't want you," commanded Hare sternly.

Little Grey Rabbit came trotting in from the garden.

"Oh, Hare! What have I done? What's the matter?" Her ears drooped and a tear came to her eye. Why was there such a mystery? Why were Squirrel and Hare always whispering?

Squirrel stamped her little foot.

"Hare! How stupid you are!"

She wiped Grey Rabbit's eyes with her tail and then spoke kindly to the gentle little animal.

"Grey Rabbit! Please will you take a bottle of primrose wine to Wise Owl? He was hooting last night. Moldy Warp would like a visit, and I am sure Fuzzypeg would love to hear a story."

"Mrs. Hedgehog would like a chat, and Robin the Postman wants someone to sort his letters," added Hare.

"Then I'll run off at once," said Grey Rabbit, smiling

up at her two friends. She trotted to the larder for an apple-pie for Mole, a bottle of primrose wine for Wise Owl, a sugar-plum for Fuzzypeg, and a slice of ginger-bread for Mrs. Hedgehog.

"Good-bye! Don't hurry back," called Squirrel and Hare, and they waved their paws as Grey Rabbit pattered along the lane to visit her friends.

"Quickly! Quickly!" cried Hare, and they bounded into the house. They danced round the kitchen carrying the mixing bowl, the egg-beater, the wooden spoon and the honey jar.

"Ha! Ha! I'm a champion cake-maker," shouted Hare, and he beat a tattoo on the flour bin with the wooden spoon.

Squirrel sprang on the dresser and sniffed at all the little pots and jars of spices and herbs.

"Here's tansy and woodruff, and preserved violets, and sugared lily-bells, and bottled cherries," said she.

"And here's fern-seed, and poppy-seed, and acorns and beech-nuts," said Hare. "Oh, here's the sugar-pot. How much shall I put in?"

"A fistful of everything makes a nice cake," said Squirrel.

So Squirrel and Hare dipped their paws into every jar, and they mixed the seeds and herbs in the yellow bowl.

"Is the oven hot?" said a deep voice, and they both sprang round in alarm. There at the window was old Hedgehog, watching them with twinkling eyes.

"I comed with extra milk for the cake," said he. "You didn't ought to forget the oven, and you didn't ought to put pepper in the cake."

"There isn't pepper in it," said Squirrel, but Hare blushed and tried to hide the pepper-pot.

"Oh, Hare! How could you! We shall have to begin all over again, and Grey Rabbit will get home before we've done."

"Never mind," said Hedgehog. "Grey Rabbit's at our house, telling tales to Fuzzypeg, and I'll go straight home and tell her about a fairy I once saw in our apple tree."

"Tell me! Tell me!" cried Hare, leaping over the dishes, and sprinkling pepper over the room.

"Atishoo! Keep calm, Hare. You've enough to do to make the cake. I'll come and lend a hand for a few minutes, and then I must be off to catch Grey Rabbit before she leaves."

So Hedgehog made up the fire and gave Hare the blow-bellows to puff the flames. He showed Squirrel how to mix the flour and butter together, and how to sprinkle in the currants and spices. Then Hare ran out into the garden and brought in rose-petals and violets and dew-drops, and pinks and clover, all the sweet-smelling things he could find to add to the cake.

He beat up the eggs till they were a yellow froth, and Hedgehog dropped them into the mixture.

"Now I must be off," said Hedgehog. "I must run

double-quick. Don't forget to butter your cake tin, and remember to keep the oven door shut. Don't open it till the good rich smell comes out."

He nodded to Hare, and gave Squirrel a pat on her bushy red tail, and away he went to find Grey Rabbit and to keep her entertained with his story of a real live fairy.

They popped the cake in the hot oven and shut the door, and Hare sat down to watch beside it. After a time there came a strong sweet smell which made Hare wrinkle his nose.

"The cake! It's talking to us! It's telling us it's ready to come out," he cried. "Quick, Squirrel! It's talking!"

So Squirrel wrapped a cloth round her paw and lifted out the good-smelling cake, as brown as a berry, all puffed up and crinkly with sugar and spices.

They carried it to the garden and hid it under an empty bee-hive. Then they swept up the floor and washed the bowl and the egg-beater.

"Aren't you tired with all this work, Squirrel?" asked Hare in a weary voice.

"Yes. I've never done so much before," murmured Squirrel.

They both dropped into their chairs, and in a minute they were fast asleep. There Grey Rabbit found them. Squirrel was clasping the wooden spoon, and Hare slept with his head on the egg-beater.

The next day, when Grey Rabbit had gone out to

gather knitting-wool from the hedges, ready for Hare's new waistcoat, Squirrel ran to the garden for the cake. She iced it, and then she wrote "GREY RABBIT'S BIRTHDAY" on the top in pollen dust. Hare put lots of candles round the edge. He went to the cupboard and took out every candle he could find, big candles, little candles, red and blue and green ones.

"Won't Grey Rabbit be surprised when she sees how old she is!" said he gaily. "A hundred years old nearly. I can't count them all, I get mixed up after seven."

They stuck little flowers in all the spaces they could find, and then they danced for joy.

"How clever we are! Who would guess we had made this! It is fit for a fairy queen," they told each other.

They hid the cake in the beehive again, ready for Midsummer Day.

"I shall give her a special present," boasted Squirrel.

"So shall I," said Hare quickly.

"A bit of a rainbow," said Squirrel.

"A star out of the sky," said Hare.

"Silly! We can't climb up to get them," said Squirrel.

"No, we can't," agreed Hare. "We must think of something else."

"I will ask the green woodpecker or the goldfinch for a few feathers, and I'll make a little fan for her," said Squirrel.

"And I will make a purse for her," said Hare.

Squirrel went to the birds and begged for a few

feathers. She put them together, and there was the prettiest little fan of green and gold.

Hare went to the pasture for a puff-ball. He squeezed out the dust, and washed the little bag in the dew. Then he filled it with rabbit-money from the hedge, and he tied it with ribbon-grasses.

Many a little animal was making a present for Grey Rabbit's birthday. Little paws were twisting rushes into baskets and carving wood-nuts, and threading flowers on strings ready for Midsummer Day. The night before the birthday they sat up to finish their work. Mole was polishing his box, Hedgehog was wrapping his gift in a dock leaf, the Speckledy Hen was burying hers in the hay lest the farm men should find it. Water-rat was down in the reed-bed among the water-lilies working by the light of the moon. Even Wise Owl had something for Grey Rabbit, and he carried his treasure under his wing when he went hunting.

Darkness came and the three little animals took their candles and went upstairs to bed. In the night Grey Rabbit was wakened by a faint noise under her window. It was a little sighing sound like the moaning of the leaves in the wind. She sat up and listened. Her eyes were wide open, and she drew the blanket up to her chin. Leaves don't sob and murmur "Oh – oh – Grey Rabbit."

She leapt out of bed and slipped her cloak over her nightgown. She ran softly downstairs and out into the garden.

There, crouched by the lavender bush in a sad little prickly ball, was Fuzzypeg. His pyjamas were drenched with dew, his eyes were wet with tears, and his prickles were shaking with sobs.

"What's the matter, little Fuzzypeg?" whispered Grey Rabbit, stooping over him.

"I comed to say Happy Birthday," sobbed Fuzzypeg. "I got out of the window and climbed down the rain-barrel. Oh! Oh! I runned very fast, but I got frightened by the rustles of the night-beasts, and I heard Wise Owl hooting."

"Poor little Fuzzypeg," said Grey Rabbit softly.

"I'm cold, Grey Rabbit," sighed Fuzzypeg.

"Come into my bed, Fuzzypeg. You'll feel better in the morning," said Grey Rabbit. She lifted up the little hedgehog and kissed his nose and dried his eyes. Then she took his paw and led him upstairs. He leapt into the pretty bed and sat looking around the room.

"Isn't it nice!" he cried. "I'm glad I comed. I knew you'd take care of me, Grey Rabbit. It's nice and warm in your bed. A Happy Birthday, Grey Rabbit."

"It isn't my birthday yet, Fuzzypeg. Not till to-morrow," said Grey Rabbit.

She wrapped him up in a couple of blankets. Then she draped the cloak around herself and crept under the bed. She couldn't sleep with a bundle of prickles by her side. She could hear the little hedgehog bouncing about in the bed above her.

"Grey Rabbit. Is it to-morrow?" he called.

Far away they could hear the church clock strike midnight, and Wise Owl flew over the house.

"A happy birthday," said Fuzzypeg quickly, as the clock finished striking. He was just in time, for Wise Owl hooted down the chimney:

"Too-whit, Too-whoo-oo,
   Happy Birthday to you-oo-oo."

"I said it first," cried Fuzzypeg, and contentedly he fell asleep.

The next morning Hare and Squirrel raced downstairs to get the breakfast. They filled the kettle and lighted the fire and made some toast. They washed the lettuce and radishes, and put a pat of butter on the table.

"I'm going to say Happy Birthday to Grey Rabbit," said Hare.

"So am I," said Squirrel.

"I shall say it first, because I'm bigger than you," said Hare.

"No, I shall say it first, because I'm the little one," said Squirrel.

They stared crossly at each other.

"Let's both say it together," said Squirrel. "I shall count, 'One, two, three, and away,' and we'll both say 'Happy Birthday, Grey Rabbit.'"

So upstairs they bundled, and they flung open the bedroom door. The bed was humped rather high with the small hedgehog who was hidden under the clothes. Grey Rabbit was fast asleep out of sight.

"One, two, three, and away!" said Squirrel.

"A Happy Birthday," came squeaking from the bedclothes before Hare could open his mouth.

Squirrel and Hare looked at each other. "Grey Rabbit's voice is very queer," stammered Squirrel.

"*You* haven't to say it, Grey Rabbit," said Hare. "*We* say it not you." He gave the humped bedclothes a hard pat.

"Oh-oo-oo!" he shrieked, leaping back and nearly knocking Squirrel over. "Grey Rabbit's grown prickles in the night."

Out of the cocoon of blankets came little Fuzzypeg's dark head.

"Hello," said he. "Good morning. I said it first."

"Oh dear me! Who's this? Who's in Grey Rabbit's bed? Why, it's Fuzzypeg!"

The noise wakened Grey Rabbit and she crawled out.

"Oh, Fuzzypeg dear, I quite forgot I was under the bed."

Hare and Squirrel were so much surprised they never said "Happy Birthday" at all. They just stared and stared.

"Milk-o! Milk-o!" The call came from the kitchen. "Has anyone seen our Fuzzypeg? He runned away in the night, and it's my belief he came to find Miss Grey Rabbit."

"Here he is, Hedgehog," the animals shouted, and they all ran helter-skelter downstairs.

"I said it first," boasted Fuzzypeg, dancing round his father. "I said 'Happy Birthday' before any of you."

"He said he would be the first and he's done it," said old Hedgehog proudly. "My! He's a bright young fellow-my-lad."

"Let him stay for breakfast," pleaded Grey Rabbit, and Hedgehog agreed. Little Fuzzypeg made some more toast and Grey Rabbit ran upstairs again to get dressed. Soon they all sat round the table and ate the nice food.

"It's your birthday, Grey Rabbit," said Squirrel, "so you shall have a holiday. We'll wash up the cups and plates and make the beds."

"Then I'll go into the garden with Fuzzypeg and show him the flowers," said Grey Rabbit. They went along the path, laughing and talking.

They came to the beehive at the garden end. Out of the little door flew a stream of honey-bees, and into the door flew another stream of bees.

"That's strange," said Grey Rabbit. "It was an empty hive."

"Honey-bees have come to live there," said Fuzzypeg.

"Hare! Squirrel! Come here! A swarm of bees is living in our empty hive," called Grey Rabbit, running to the house. "Isn't it exciting?"

"Oh! Oh! Oh!" cried Squirrel and Hare. "Oh dear me! What shall we do?"

"Aren't you glad?" asked Grey Rabbit, surprised.

"It's a cal-al-am-ity," said Hare, and Squirrel burst into tears.

"Listen," said Grey Rabbit, putting her arm round Squirrel.

The bees were humming something and this is what the animals heard:

> "It's Grey Rabbit's Birthday,
>   She doesn't want money,
>   Or fine clothes or riches.
>   We'll make her some honey."

"Kind little creatures," said Grey Rabbit, but Hare and Squirrel looked at one another and sighed.

"Honey out of our cake," they whispered.

Grey Rabbit took Fuzzypeg home, and when she returned the work was all done. They sat in the garden, and told tales and sang songs, but Squirrel and Hare were anxious about the party. There would be no cake, only honey for the guests.

At four o'clock they sent Grey Rabbit upstairs to put on her clean collar and cuffs, while they got ready the tea.

They ran down the garden to the bee-skep for the honey. Hare put on his Home Guard gas-mask lest he should be stung, but the bees had gone. They lifted up the straw skep, and behold! there was the cake looking nicer than ever, and around it were many little pots of honey, each as big as a thimble.

The pots were made of golden wax, and the honey was scented with wild thyme.

They carried the treasures indoors, and placed them round the table, with the cake in the middle.

"There'll be a pot for everybody, and some left over," said Hare, smacking his lips.

They called Grey Rabbit and she came running downstairs.

What a surprise there was! The table was beautiful with the birthday cake and all the candles alight upon it. The tiny pots of honey shone like gold, and there were dishes of cresses and nuts and cream.

"Oh! Oh!" cried Grey Rabbit. "What's this?"

"It's somebody's birthday cake," said Squirrel.

"It's everybody's cake, and here they come to the feast," said Hare.

Up the path came many little feet. Voices were chattering and whispering and squeaking with excitement. Then there was a rat-tat-tat at the door.

"Come in! Come in!" cried Squirrel.

In trooped Moldy Warp, Hedgehog and Mrs. Hedgehog and Fuzzypeg, Water-rat and the Speckledy Hen and a crowd of little animals.

"Many happy returns, Grey Rabbit," they cried. They saw the table and the lighted cake and the honey-pots.

"Oh-oh-oh-oh! It's like Moldy Warp's Christmas

tree."

Squirrel gave Grey Rabbit the little green-and-gold fan made of feathers of the woodpecker and goldfinch.

Hare brought out the purse of rabbit-money tied with green ribbon grass. The Speckledy Hen placed a cream cheese wrapped in a nut-leaf on the table. Old Hedgehog gave Grey Rabbit a pot of elderflower salve. Mrs. Hedgehog gave her a new white pocket handkerchief with G. R. in the corner. Fuzzypeg had a basket which he had made out of a brown chestnut.

He had filled it with tiny violets and pimpernels for his friend. Water-rat brought a little canoe on his back so that Grey Rabbit could paddle over the muddy rain-pools. Rat stood in the doorway with a candlestick he had carved out of a bone. It was just big enough to hold a rush-light. Every little rabbit brought something.

There were bedroom slippers and bunches of roses and door-mats of rushes, and toys and games for Grey Rabbit.

Moldy Warp's present was the best of all. It was the song of a nightingale, in a tiny polished musical box.

They were all listening to the music as Grey Rabbit turned the handle, when there was a flurry and rush at the door. They all fell over one another as the door was pushed open and a round feathered head and a pair of large blinking eyes appeared.

"I won't come in," hooted Wise Owl in his wailing voice. "No, I don't want to discommode you, but I have

brought a small token of my regard for Grey Rabbit."

He thrust one claw forward and dropped a book on the table. Then, without waiting, he drifted away as silently as he had come.

"Whew!" exclaimed Moldy Warp. "That was a shock."

They all scrambled to their feet and dusted their clothes.

"What has he brought?" asked Hare, coming out from under the table.

"A book from his library. It's called 'Wise Owl's Guide to Knowledge,'" said Grey Rabbit, clasping the tiny green volume. "Now I can tell Fuzzypeg everything he wants to know."

"Cut the cake! Cut the cake, Grey Rabbit!" called Hare. "I'm hungry. Cut the cake!"

So Grey Rabbit cut the beautiful birthday cake and they all had a piece. It was as nice as it looked. Really, Hare and Squirrel had made it very well!

Moldy Warp drank Grey Rabbit's health, and Water-rat made a speech.

Squirrel recited a little poem, and Hare played a tune on his flute.

Then old Hedgehog told them all the story of the fairy he had seen up in the apple tree, and Mrs. Hedgehog said she had heard that tale a dozen times before.

They all laughed and sang and danced till night came, and then they went home by the light of the moon.

"What a lovely birthday it has been!" said Grey Rabbit. "How kind everybody is to me!"

She looked at her presents on the table. The musical box with the song of the nightingale, "Wise Owl's Guide to Knowledge," Robin's pin-cushion, Water-rat's canoe, the handkerchief, the tiny chestnut basket of flowers, the puff-ball purse, the bone candlestick, the feather fan, the honey-pots, and all the little treasures the woodland folk had brought.

She went upstairs to bed with the musical box under her arm. She turned the handle and the voice of the nightingale came trilling forth. From the woods another nightingale answered.

"A Happy Birthday, Grey Rabbit," it seemed to say. "Thank you for all the fun you give us, little rabbit."

The End of the Story

Little Grey Rabbit
and the Circus

Little Grey Rabbit looked out of the kitchen door early one morning, to welcome the sun and nod to the trees. The sun was in the sky and the trees were in the wood, but the sun was too busy looking at something in the field to notice Grey Rabbit. So Grey Rabbit looked too.

"It wasn't there last night. Has it grown?" she asked.

It was exactly like a large red-and-white striped mushroom.

"A mushroom or a toadstool. They come up quickly in the night," she thought. "A very pretty one."

"Hare! Squirrel!" she called. "Hare! Squirrel! Wake up and come and see."

Hare and Squirrel tumbled out of their beds and nearly fell downstairs in their hurry.

"It's a 'nor-mous toadstool, red as a poppy," said Hare.

"It's an umbrella," said Squirrel. "It's like my parasol I lost in the river on our picnic."

"We'll get dressed and go and look at it before it fades away," said Hare. "Don't go without us, Grey Rabbit."

They scampered up to their rooms, threw on some clothes and hurried back.

"Come along, follow me," cried Hare, boldly leading the way. "I'll take care of you."

They hurried through the fields, but when they approached the toadstool they went slowly, for they could see what it was. It was a tent, made of gossamer-silk, and the wind caused it to billow and sway. The folds of the tent opened and a Black Hare stepped out. He was a handsome fellow, with laughing eyes and jigging step, and he leapt and jumped towards them as if he were a dancing master.

He carried a bunch of ivy leaves, and a hazel stick with some wild flowers fastened to the top.

"Good morning, Hare, Squirrel and Little Grey Rabbit," said he, bowing and leaping towards the three. He offered his green stick to Grey Rabbit.

"We have pitched our tent in your field, Grey Rabbit, and we will pay you a day's rent of a pinch of fern seed. Here is a free pass to our circus."

Grey Rabbit took the hazel stick, but she was rather nervous of this prancing Hare.

"Circus, sir Hare?" she stammered.

"I am the leader of our circus. We have travelled the

land, we have acted in meadow and copse, on heath and common, in bog and on moorland. We have even danced before Kings and Queens," said the Black Hare, proudly.

"Kings and Queens?" echoed Grey Rabbit.

"Well, King-fishers and Queen Bees," explained the Black Hare.

"King-cups and Queen-of-the-meadows," added Squirrel.

"King of Hearts and Queen of Spades," said Hare, who had played Snap with the Fox.

"Yes, all those Kings and Queens," said the Black Hare. "And now we have come to your home to show you our dances and tricks."

"Oh! oh! thank you," cried Squirrel, Hare and Grey Rabbit.

"This is a treat in a quiet place where we never hear a song except that of the blackbird and throstle and nightingale, and we never see any magic except Wise Owl's tricks," said Hare.

"Do you know Wise Owl?" asked Grey Rabbit.

"I've heard of him. I am going to invite him to our performance," said the Black Hare. "But I must hurry away. I have these ivy notes to deliver to all the cottages of the woods and fields."

"Don't forget to call at Moldy Warp's hill," shouted Hare. "You might miss it."

"And at Water Rat's, down by the river," added

Squirrel.

"And please invite Mr. and Mrs. Rat and their baby," said little Grey Rabbit. "Nobody asks them to anything."

"But *don't* invite the Weasels," said Squirrel and Hare.

The Black Hare promised he would not call on the Weasels, and then away he went, fairly galloping over the field, so that Hare stared after him with envy.

"There's writing on this ivy-leaf," said Grey Rabbit, "but I cannot read it. Can you, Fuzzypeg?"

Fuzzypeg held the letter close to his nose.

"It says 'Dances, Tricks, Clowns'."

They all ran indoors and made the breakfast, talking excitedly about the circus.

Hare burned the toast, and Squirrel dropped the new-laid egg on the floor and Grey Rabbit made the tea without putting any tea in the pot. Even Fuzzypeg caught his spikes on the table-cloth and dragged it off the table.

Then Old Hedgehog came to the door with the milk.

"Milk-o! Milk-o!" he cried. "Have you seen it? There's a travelling show with a tent outside in the field. Have you seen the sight, Miss Grey Rabbit and Miss Squirrel?"

Then he spied little Fuzzypeg sitting wrapped up in the tablecloth trying to disentangle his prickles.

"There you are, Fuzzypeg! Up to mischief! Your mother is looking for you," said he severely; but his eyes

brightened with joy as he looked at the little Hedgehog.

"We know all about the tent," said Hare, in a lordly way. "There's the Black Hare and his circus, and the Seven Clowns."

"Seven!" cried Hedgehog. "Seven, same as the stars in the Great Bear?"

"What are clowns?" asked Squirrel.

"Animals like me and you," piped Fuzzypeg.

"We are going to see them this afternoon," said Grey Rabbit, happily.

"Oh, my!" Hedgehog blinked his eyes and rattled his quills and stamped his little feet in a clog dance. "What a stir in our countryside! What a to-do in the fields! Nay, I've never heard tell of such a thing since the cow jumped over the moon."

"You must bring Mrs. Hedgehog," said Hare.

"She will bring me," said Old Hedgehog." "Fuzzypeg's here all ready to go along of you."

Throughout the morning many little animals came peeping through the bushes, creeping along the paths in the thick grass, peering at the red-and-white tent among the buttercups. Some rabbits brought their dinners and sat waiting for the performance to begin. A family of field mice carried a hamper of food and sat on it. Squirrels swung from the trees and frogs hopped in the wet ditches. All wanted to be in time, and they watched the sun move up the sky and the shadows shorten. At twelve o'clock the shadows are the shortest of all, as every animal knows, so they had their dinners.

The Speckledy Hen came clucking up with a basket of eggs. Water Rat appeared in his best velvet coat with clean ruffles, and his housekeeper Mrs. Webster brought a few cakes for the hungry ones.

Squirrel, Hare and little Grey Rabbit in their best clothes joined the gathering. The Rat with his wife and baby stood in the distance, waiting by the ferny hollow, where the frogs were chattering. Wise Owl sat sleepily yawning in a tree near the tent.

At last the tent door opened and everybody stopped talking.

The Black Hare stepped out, He wore a ruff round his neck and he carried an ebony stick and a little silver bell, and a banner.

"Walk up! Come closer!" he called, and he rang the bell. "Don't be afraid. Take your seats on the grass."

The animals came near. They squatted on the sloping bank by the tent, where they could get a good view.

"My friends," said the Black Hare, bowing low. "May I present to you the artistes in my circus?"

He drew back the folds of the tent and from its shadows came a magnificent black and green Cock with a long sweeping tail.

"That's our Cockadoodle, who ran away from the farm," whispered the Speckledy Hen.

"Hush!" said the Black Hare.

Next came a rabbit, brushed and shining, with a

round little face and twitching ears. She bent her pretty head and made a curtsey to the audience. She was white as new-fallen snow.

"This is Snow-white," said the Black Hare, "and here are the seven clowns."

Seven fat little dormice rolled on the grass and twisted themselves into knots as they tumbled about like small brown clowns.

The snow rabbit stood there in her flower-petal skirt, and then she danced.

"Is she real?" asked Fuzzypeg.

The Black Hare turned to him. "You may well ask, my little Hedgehog," said he. "She is the prettiest rabbit in the world. She won a prize at the County Show, but she was unhappy in her hutch. She was a prisoner like all of us – for I was a captive, too. We escaped, and then the dormice joined us and the Cock flew to us from the farm.

"Here we are to amuse you. We sing our songs and perform our tricks and we live in a tent which was woven for us by all the gossamer spiders."

He bowed, and everyone cheered and stamped so that there was a noise like the wind, with soft feet drumming on the grass and little bodies rustling to and fro. The Fox heard the sound, but when he came towards the circle of animals there was an invisible barrier which no savage creature could get through. It had been made by the Black Hare who had spilled fern seed all round to protect the circus.

"The Cock will open with a song," said the Black
Hare. The Cock stepped forward, and sang:

"Cock-a-doodle-doo.
    We've brought our play to you.
    We sing and dance
    And lightly prance
    To wish you how-d'ye-do."

His shrill cock-a-doodle carried over the fields to the
farmyard. "There, listen! Do you hear him? I wish he
would come back," said the Hens.

Next the Black Hare leapt through a hoop which the
Cock held and all the little dormice leapt after him. He
climbed a ladder and balanced on the top rung and they
climbed too. He walked along a tightrope of rushes
which was stretched between two trees. He tumbled
head over heels on the grass so fast he looked like a ball of
sooty fur, and the dormice rolled after him.

"Splendid," cried Hare, leaping up. "I shall try to do
those tricks myself."

Little Grey Rabbit sat with her eyes wide open,
longing to be a beautiful white rabbit with long snowy
fur and a flower-petal dress. She looked at her own little
grey dress and blue apron, and she sighed. Hare was
gazing at the Black Hare, wishing he could be like him.
Fuzzypeg laughed at the dormice, rolling about like
clowns all the time. He knew he could roll, but he couldn't
spin through the grass like those little balls. Squirrel was

whispering to the Speckledy Hen.

"Yes, dear Speckledy Hen. He is a beautiful Cock. I wish he would return to your farmyard."

"Yes, dear Squirrel, I do wish he would," sighed the Speckledy Hen.

"Can anyone lend me a watch?" asked the Black Hare, stepping among the animals with an air of importance. Each one shuffled and felt in his pocket. Even Wise Owl, up the tree, felt in his feathers, but nobody had a watch except Hare.

"I'll lend you mine," said Hare, proudly holding up the turnip watch which kept such queer time.

The Black Hare took it in his paw, and held it dangling by its chain for all to see and admire. "Twelve o'clock," said the Black Hare, then: "Presto. Pass!" he added, and at the magical words the watch disappeared.

It was nowhere. It had completely gone. Poor Hare looked very sad, and Grey Rabbit had to comfort him.

"What is that on top of yonder beech tree?" asked the Black Hare, and they all looked skywards. Some thought they saw the watch dangling there, and others said it was Wise Owl. Squirrel offered to go up and look for it, but the Black Hare shook his head.

"No, Miss Squirrel," said he. "I will call it down."

"Come down from yonder tree! Come along here!" he commanded. Then he added: "Will you now feel in your pocket, Mister Hare?"

Hare put his hand in his pocket and there was the

turnip watch. It said 1 o'clock.

"I can do better than that," hooted Wise Owl. "I can make the watch disappear and never come back."

"Not to-day, sir. Not to-day," said the Black Hare, hurriedly, and Wise Owl shrugged his shoulders.

The Black Hare then produced yards of daisy chains from Grey Rabbit's apron-pocket, and a flock of butterflies from Squirrel's dress.

He whistled and a swallow-tail flew from Fuzzypeg's smock, and a red admiral from Mrs. Hedgehog's umbrella.

In the Mole's pocket was an acorn, which he broke open to show a fairy tree.

In the Water Rat's frills a humble-bee played a tune.

Even Wise Owl, up in the tree, frowning and blinking his eyes, even Wise Owl was caught in the magic of that Black Hare, for from under his wing there came a bit-bat which zig-zagged away.

Marvellous! Wonderful! Everyone was astonished at the conjuring tricks of the Black Hare.

"Thank you, dear friends, for your patronage," said the Black Hare.

"Three cheers for the Black Hare, the Snow Rabbit, the Cock and the Dormice," said Mole, and everyone waved and cried, "Hurrah!"

It was nearly dusk when some of them reached home. The tent was closed and all was quiet.

In the early morning Squirrel looked out of her

window, and saw an empty field. Quickly she got up and dressed. She packed a little bag with her nightgown and her teazel brush, and slipped quietly downstairs and ran across the common following the trail of the circus.

Hare also looked out of his window. He, too, dressed and followed the travelling show, with his watch and his flute.

Then Grey Rabbit awoke and looked out. She dressed and ran downstairs. She seized her cloak and put on her goloshes, and followed the track in the dewy field.

When she got to the top of the hill she could see far away the little red-and-white tent carried by the Black Hare, while the White Rabbit and the Dormice trotted behind. Then she saw Hare, lolloping along and Squirrel racing after.

"We are all running away from home," she said. "We are all running away. Oh! how foolish we are."

The Cock leaned out from a tree and spoke to her.

"I am not running away, Grey Rabbit. I am going back to the farm, to see dear old Speckledy Hen again. They will have to carry on without me."

"Oh, I am glad you are going back to Speckledy Hen," said Grey Rabbit.

"I can see Squirrel and Hare over there. They are turning round. They are coming home," continued the Cock.

Sure enough Hare and Squirrel caught up with them before they got home, and they had a merry breakfast together.

"Good-bye, Grey Rabbit," called the Cock as he set off to the farmyard. "Good-bye. I shall see you again soon."

"I nearly joined that circus," said Hare.

"So did I," said Squirrel.

"We all nearly ran away," laughed Grey Rabbit. "But home is best."

The End of the Story

LITTLE GREY RABBIT'S STORYBOOK

by Alison Uttley

PICTURES BY
MARGARET TEMPEST

Little Grey Rabbit's Party

Wise Owl's Story

Little Grey Rabbit's Washing Day

Moldy Warp the Mole

Fuzzypeg Goes to School

Little Grey Rabbit's Christmas

The first anthology of Little Grey Rabbit stories with Margaret Tempest's original paintings reproduced afresh was enthusiastically received everywhere.

"Here, nearly half a century after the first Grey Rabbit book appeared, is the first 'anthology', six favourite tales in one fine volume with all the pictures looking as if they had just been painted."

The Good Book Guide

"What a joy to find a collection of the Little Grey Rabbit stories nicely printed on glossy paper with beautiful illustrations!"

Nursery World

"The stories of Grey Rabbit, Hare, Fuzzypeg and Squirrel are full of homely country details and this collection makes a most attractive gift for children of 4–8."

Children's Book Newsletter